THE KING
KILLERS

BOOKS BY THOMAS B. DEWEY

The "Mac" series:

Draw the Curtain Close
Every Bet's a Sure Thing
Prey for Me
The Mean Streets
The Brave, Bad Girls
You've Got Him Cold
The Case of the Chased and the Chaste
The Girl Who Wasn't There
How Hard to Kill
A Sad Song Singing
Don't Cry for Long
Portrait of a Dead Heiress
Deadline
Death and Taxes
The King Killers
The Love-Death Thing
The Taurus Trip

The Pete Schoefield Series

And When She Stops
Go To Sleep, Jeannie
Too Hot For Hawaii
The Golden Hooligan
Go, Honeylou
The Girl With The Sweet Plump Knees
The Girl in the Punchbowl
Only on Tuesdays
Nude in Nevada

The Singer Batts Series

Hue and Cry
As Good As Dead
Mourning After
Handle with Fear

Others Novels

My Love Is Violent
Hunter at Large
Can a Mermaid Kill?
A Season of Violence

THE KING KILLERS

THOMAS B. DEWEY

WILDSIDE PRESS

CHAPTER 1

Karl Schneider and I were in the same business, and I suppose we had certain characteristics in common, but resemblances are deceiving, and I would not like to be taken for him in any profound sense. Nor, I'm sure, would he care to be taken for me. We were thrown together by accident, and the adventures we shared, though bizarre and sometimes violent, were thrust upon us and provided thin basis for a permanent relationship.

It started late in the afternoon of a sticky summer day, in the office of a man named Nat Pines, a commission merchant for whom I worked from time to time. Nat was a good thing for my business, but it was tough on him that he had to call on me as often as he did. He dealt in some odd commodities, and when you're buying and selling offbeat items, the chances are your customers are a little odd too. Nat could collect past-due bills with the best of us, but there were times when, for policy reasons, he'd want a professional outsider like me. This was one of the times.

"You could have fooled me good," he said. "These people are well heeled, and before, every deal came through bang-bang, right on time. Now they're ninety days behind, and I'm sweating."

"How much?" I asked him.

"Four-five," he said. "I already paid for the merchandise. I'm out three."

He was talking in thousands. Nat wasn't a big dealer, but he was consistent, and $3,000 made a difference to him.

"You tried getting it on your own?"

"Oh, sure. Half a dozen phone calls in the last couple weeks. I don't understand it. They been good every time till now."

"What kind of merchandise?" I asked.

"Guns," he said. "Sidepieces."

I blinked at him.

"You selling to the army now?"

"No. They're not real. Toys. Wooden guns."

"Forty-five hundred dollars' worth of toy guns?"

Nat shrugged.

"I don't ask what they want them for. If they can buy, I can sell."

"It's all right with me," I said. "What do we have for a name and address?"

"That's another thing," he said. "It's a California outfit, but right now they got all their big shots here in town. So maybe that's convenient."

"It's more convenient, let's say, than if they were in California and I had to go out there."

"Yeah," Nat said.

Nat never had much sense of humor. Money was not a funny thing. You could say for him, though, that he was as serious about other people's money as he was about his own.

He pushed a thin sheaf of invoices and past-due notices across his desk, and I picked it up. The top sheet was stamped FINAL NOTICE, dated two weeks previous, and was addressed to LEAGUE FOR GOOD GOVERN-MENT, in a town I had never heard of in California.

I looked through the earlier invoices, notices and memoranda on which Nat had scribbled his own notes on his efforts to collect.

"There's a signed receipt in here?" I asked.

"Yeah, somewhere. The stuff was delivered all right—and signed for." He took to scratching the side of his thin neck. "But it's a different guy."

"Is the delivery receipt good for an O.K.?"

"It always was before," Nat said.

I found the delivery receipt. It specified a delivery of twelve hundred handguns, at the address I had seen on the later notice, and it was signed, as nearly as I could make out, by a man named Henry Feeding, or Fielding. "What was the signature before this?" I asked.

"Royal," he said. "Nick Royal."

"Maybe they're going through reorganization."

"Maybe," he said, "but this guy, Fielding or whatever it is, he's the top man. His O.K. ought to be the true word."

A Chicago address had been written in Nat's hand at the bottom of the final notice. It was one of the older buildings on LaSalle Street.

"All right," I said, getting up. "I'll give it a shot. What kind of an organization is it?"

Nat looked away and scratched harder at his neck.

"I don't know—one of those right-wing things—like the Minutemen, you know. California's full of that crap."

"Like Nazis?" I said, watching him.

He scratched the neck.

"I sell stuff," he said. "One guy's money is like anybody else's."

"I thought those outfits used real guns," I said.

Nat shrugged some more.

"You can get in trouble with real guns—with the government," he said.

"Yeah," I said.

I reset my hat and turned to the door, then looked back.

"By the way, what are they doing here? How did you know they were in town?"

"It was in the paper," he said. "I don't know about this Nick Royal, whoever he is, but the big shot, Fielding, and some of his staff—I forget the names. It was in the paper."

"Just a news item?"

"Yeah, a little thing. I happened to notice it."

"Was this address in the paper, too?"

"No, I had to find that. No sweat. I called the hotel, and they gave me the office address."

"What hotel?"

"Palmer House. That's where they're staying."

"That's where you made your latest calls?"

"Just one. I talked to some dame. She was pretty snotty. I decided not to bug 'em."

"All right, Nat," I said. "I'll bug 'em."

"Thanks, Mac," he said. "You can call me at home."

"Sure."

I left him, went down to my car and drove over to LaSalle Street. It wasn't much of a drive.

* * * *

On a black and white directory in the Indiana limestone lobby of the old office building, I found the name LEAGUE FOR GOOD GOVERN-MENT—ROOM 1208. Under the main heading was the name, EDGAR ROYAL. Nat Pines had mentioned a Nick Royal. If Edgar and Nick were the same man, it would be a help. But probably they were not the same. Few things work out so neatly in my business.

The elevator throbbed upward slowly, and I looked through my sheaf of papers while I rode it out. The original invoice, the first and oldest item, was in good order and had been stamped "Rec'd. April 16." That was over three months past. The delivery receipt, signed by Henry Fielding, had been received three or four days later. Nothing unusual about that. When Nat was informed by his supplier that shipment had been made, he would send out the invoice. I turned the delivery receipt over and looked at the back of it. The name "Nick" had been written in longhand; then a pencil line had been drawn through it, and there was a note in a different hand: "Ref. to Mr. F." Still nothing unusual. The item had been referred to the top man in the organization. He had signed the delivery receipt. That was all to the good and ought to make collection—or suit, if necessary—easier. There were no marks on the rest of the items, except those Nat had scribbled, and I put the sheaf in my pocket and got off at the twelfth floor. I wasn't hopeful. My conception of groups like the League for Good Government was of a few ill-mannered, disheveled persons, carrying fat briefcases stuffed with crank- and hate-sheets. Never any money.

Nothing happened to change my conception until I walked into the outer office, on whose frosted door panel was lettered the name LEAGUE FOR GOOD GOVERNMENT. Then my impression changed, not because of any display of opulence, but because of the receptionist-secretary behind the large well-tended desk. The desk was big enough to take up a full third of the space. Still, the girl was in command. She looked good like a California girl should.

She had a high pile of sun-bleached golden hair, and golden eyebrows. She was full-bodied but well proportioned, dressed in a miniskirt, her bare feet under the desk. There was a pair of sandals under the desk, too, but she didn't have them on her feet, which were tanned and serviceable-looking. She smiled at me, showing strong white teeth.

"What may I do for you?" she asked.

"I'd like to see whoever is in charge," I said.

"Mr. Edgar Royal is in charge," she said. "He's busy at the moment. May I tell him who's calling?"

I hauled up on my fascination with her and attended to the preparation for getting past her—no small feat for a bill collector in any situation.

"I represent a client," I said, "who has an interest in the League for Good Government."

That was fairly accurate, I told myself. Nat Pines had at least a $4,500 interest in the League.

"Can you tell me your client's name?" she asked.

"I'd rather not at the moment," I said. "He's a well-known figure, and I—"

"I understand," she said, making a brisk note on a beige scratch pad.

She got up and headed into the inner office, her miniskirt riding high on her tanned thighs. I was glad it was summer. When she came back, she smiled some more, but in a routine, perfunctory way, and let me watch her settle down to some typing. She typed at a smart, no-nonsense clip, using all her fingers. Sometimes her nice red lips twisted slightly. I didn't mind waiting.

Unhappily, I didn't get to wait long. A buzzer rang. The blond goddess rose, looked into the next office, came back and said, "Mr. Royal will see you now."

"Thank you," I said, and walked past her into Edgar Royal's office.

He sat straight in his chair at a steel desk piled with pamphlets and brochures. He was well set up, about my size, with black hair cut short. He had a purple birthmark that ran from his left lower cheek down onto his neck. He wore glasses with big tortoiseshell rims, and his eyes behind them looked larger than normal: smallish intent pupils with a lot of white space around them. His jaw was tight and didn't move much when he talked, as if he had broken it at some time and it had never set properly. He had small, almost effeminate hands, but he kept them fairly quiet. He was used to meeting people. I wondered how many bill collectors he had had to deal with. "Something we can do for you?" he said.

"I hope so," I said. "I represent a man named Nat Pines. He sold you a shipment of handguns."

His intense pupils rested at ease in their white disks. "Yes?" he said.

"And he hasn't been paid for them yet," I said, "and inasmuch as delivery was made more than three months ago, he feels entitled to ask for his money."

"You have a delivery receipt?" he asked. "Have we O.K.'d the invoice?"

"Right here," I said.

I detached the two items he had asked for and put them on his desk. He moved only his hands, examining the documents. After a moment he reached for a buzzer. The girl answered from the front office, and Royal asked her to get Mr. Fielding on the telephone. While he waited, he said, "My brother Nick usually handles these things. I don't see his name here."

"His name—anyway the name 'Nick'—is on the back of the delivery receipt, but it's crossed out. The receipt is signed by Mr. Fielding."

"I see it is," he said.

You never know about these things. They can play it cool till you practically feel the money in your hand, then suddenly snarl like a nervous dog and throw you out. And they've got a right to throw you out, unless there's a law officer with you.

The buzzer sounded, and Royal lifted the phone.

"Hello... Oh, Gretchen. He isn't there?"

He listened for some time, his eyes cool behind his glasses.

"All right, I'll take care of that later. There's a man here about the payment for those guns—three months ago. What happened?... Nick told you not to pay it? Why?... I see. Well, Mr. Fielding O.K.'d it. What shall I tell him?... All right. Will you ask Fielding to call me when he comes in?... Yes, all right."

He hung up and turned slightly in his chair. The only change in him was a tightening around the mouth. It began to look like a fight.

"There's a question about the shipment," Royal said. "I can't help you from here."

"I don't know what that means exactly," I said. "What's the question on the shipment?"

"The guns were defective."

I stared at him. Everything had turned unreal.

"The guns were made of wood," I said. "How could they be defective?"

He moved his hands.

"I don't know. It's not my department. My brother Nick is in charge of that and he advised that the invoice not be paid."

"Where can I see your brother Nick?"

"He's in California."

More and more unreal. A problem of collecting less than $5,000 for a load of defective wooden guns delivered to California! I felt like a babe in toyland.

"I think I had better talk to Mr. Fielding," I said.

"Very doubtful Mr. Fielding will see you. He's a busy man, and my brother Nick—"

"But your brother Nick is in California, and Mr. Fielding is here in town. He has a good past record with my client. I'd hate to see it get spoiled."

"If that's a threat," he said, "you're wasting it on me." So that was the end of that. Any more talk would only weaken my position. I got on my feet.

"I'll try Mr. Fielding," I said. "Palmer House, isn't it?" He didn't say anything, but I hadn't expected him to say anything. I went out fast, but slowed down as soon as the door went shut behind me, because the lovely blond barefoot lass was still at the desk and she gave me one of those smiles as I passed.

"Thank you," I said.

At the door I turned to look back at her.

"You're from California," I said.

She looked momentarily startled, then shook her gorgeous head.

"Not me," she said. "I'm from Evanston."

"Oh," I said. "Goodbye."

I got out, not without stubbing my toe lightly on the meager threshold—a failure on every count so far.

CHAPTER 2

At the Palmer House, I used a telephone in the lobby to call Nat Pines. He was at home.

"You ever get any word from Fielding or anybody that those guns were defective?" I asked him.

"Defective? No, I never—" A pause, then his voice came like a strangled scream. "Defective! How could a bunch of toy guns made out of wood be—"

"That's my question," I said. "Were they supposed to shoot anything, like wooden beebees, rubber bands—"

"Hell, no! They were turned out on lathes, for God's sake! They were supposed to look sort of like thirty-eight-caliber automatic jobs—I don't know about guns!"

"No trigger action, no movable parts?"

"Nothing like that. Who says they were defective?"

"That's the excuse they're giving. I'm on my way to see Mr. Fielding."

"O.K., good luck."

At the desk, the clerk wouldn't acknowledge the presence in his house of a Mr. Henry Fielding from California. I asked for Edgar Royal, and he shook his head.

"A lady named Gretchen?" I suggested.

He looked blank. I began to think Nat Pines had been misinformed about where they were staying or that they had moved to another hotel. I was on the point of trying heavier persuasion on the clerk when I caught sight of an acquaintance named Ed Croft, the chief hotel cop. I caught up with him in the shade of a potted palm and we shook hands. He was a large stolid guy, and long ago we had been on the police force together. He had lasted a lot longer than I, having no enemies to speak of. He was a guy it would be hard to hold a grudge against.

"How are things?" he asked.

"Fine. I got to talk to a person."

"Who?"

"Edgar Royal."

His face went sad.

"Any other room in the house, Mac. This one is off limits."

"How come? They've got a special wire to the management?"

"I don't know. I know I've got orders."

We sat there. Pretty soon I said, "Mr. Henry Fielding."

"Who?" he said.

"Come on, Ed," I said. "We're friends, remember? Remember that time you got your foot caught in the streetcar track and I—"

"All right, shut up."

I waited. He moved his eyes for a while and then said, "Fielding has a room adjoining the Royal suite. He's not registered. Officially, he's not here."

"I see," I said. "Then there can't be any orders about him, can there?"

"Now, Mac—"

"You can't have orders to maintain privacy for a man who isn't here. It wouldn't be—realistic."

"He's here, he's part of the suite—"

"But not officially."

"What are you going to do?"

"You don't really want to know, do you?"

"No, but listen—"

"Relax," I said. "I won't make any problems."

"Promise?"

"You know me."

"Yeah," he said, in a tone pregnant with meaning. "I know you good."

"Trust me," I said.

He still held out. I could see him beginning to calculate.

"This is private-eye day," he said. "How about it? I help you, you help me. O.K.?"

It was my turn to be careful.

"If I can," I said.

"There was a bird dog nosing around earlier, a guy named Schneider—Karl Schneider. You know him?"

"No. Was he nosing around after the Fielding crowd?"

"No. Somebody else. Somebody named Barnes—Ray Barnes."

"Is there a Ray Barnes in the hotel?"

"Yeah. I don't know anything about him."

"What do you want me to do?"

"Check out Karl Schneider."

"Well now, Ed, that could run into a big—"

He found a scrap of paper in his pocket.

"He left a couple of phone numbers. He wants me to call him if Barnes checks out—of the hotel, I mean."

"Did you tell him you would?"

"No. I told him I didn't know if I would or not. He left the numbers anyway."

I took the paper from his hand.

"O.K. You tell me where the Edgar Royal suite is, and I'll look into this Karl Schneider."

He looked this way and that and said, "The Royals are in nine-o-eight and ten, and Mr. Fielding is in nine-twelve."

"Who are the Royals?" I asked.

"Mr. and Mrs. Edgar Royal."

"Thanks. See you later."

I waited till he disappeared. He was a good man, and there wasn't any big worry for him. He just had to do some worrying from time to time to take care of his conscience. He was an institution man.

I went to one of the elevators and rode up to the ninth floor. The two rooms of the Royal suite were halfway along the main hall. I walked down to 908 and used the knocker. Nothing. I was at the door of 910 when the telephone rang inside. A woman's voice answered it. I decided to wait till she had finished, so as not to get her needlessly upset by interruptions. When you ask for money, you ought to be pleasant about it as long as possible.

I couldn't make out what she was saying, but I didn't try very hard. The other party seemed to be doing most of the talking. Once in a while she would say a few words, most of them negative. Finally she said, "Goodbye," and that seemed to end it. I waited for a count of three and used the knocker.

A judas window opened, and she looked out at me.

"What is it?" she said.

"I just came from Mr. Edgar Royal's office," I said.

"Yes?"

"I thought I might be able to talk with Mr. Henry Fielding."

I couldn't see anything but her eyes through the little window. They were large and cool, like Edgar Royal's. They didn't jump around any.

"Mr. Fielding is not here," she said.

"Do you expect him any time soon?"

"I don't know. What do you want to talk to him about?"

"It's about a shipment of guns," I said.

"Oh, that."

"Something was said about their being defective. I was wondering whether—"

Her telephone rang again.

"Excuse me," she said.

She went away, leaving the judas window open. It gave me a chance to have a look at her. She was forty, give or take a year, large-bodied but shapely, with honey-blond hair and a handsome, well-tended face. She was wearing a sky-blue housecoat and matching slippers. Her hand on the telephone was firm and competent.

"Hello," she said. "Yes, this is Mrs. Royal... Who? I don't know anyone named Ray Barnes. Have we met?... No, I don't know where Eloise is at the moment... That's impossible—her father is in California... What?... Well, then I assume she's in good hands... Who? Schneider? I don't know anyone named Schneider. What does he have to do with it?... I see. Then her father is taking care of everything. I'm afraid I can't help you, Mr. Barnes... Yes, goodbye."

She hung up and walked away out of sight as if she had forgotten about me. I waited a few seconds and used the knocker. She reappeared, lighting a cigarette as she came.

"You're still there?" she said. "I'm sorry, I can't do a thing for you on those guns. You'll have to talk to Mr. Fielding."

"When will Mr. Fielding be available?"

"I just don't know. Goodbye now."

She snapped the judas window shut, and I could hear her walking away from the door, her slippers whispering on the carpet.

I looked at my watch, and it read five forty-five. Eventually, Mr. Henry Fielding would have to return, if only to pick up a toothbrush. I had nothing more urgent to do, and there was $500 in it if I could collect that bill.

I walked down the hall to the transverse corridor and stood around. It could be a long wait. I could get thrown out—by good old Ed Croft himself—if I got turned in for loitering. But I had been thrown out of hotels in the past, and I was still in business. It was a calculated risk and worth taking.

Waiting time is at least three times longer than any other time, unless what you're waiting for is doom. I was waiting for a chance to make $500 and it seemed to take forever. Actually it was about twelve minutes. Two or three tenants entered or left their rooms, but nobody got nervous about me as far as I could tell. Once in a while I would take a slow walk to the dead end of the hall and back. It kept my joints greased.

At about three minutes to six I rounded the corner, returning from one of my walks, and a guy came down the main corridor, approaching the Royal suite. He was close to sixty, maybe older, but upright and taut as a physical-culture model. His hair was gray and smoothly groomed. He wore a pince-nez on a long nose, and he was dressed for the street in a tailored gray suit that must have cost him $300. About ten paces behind him came two other men, younger, well-muscled, wearing white sport shirts under loose-fitting jackets. The jackets and shirts were as identical as uniforms.

The older man stopped at the door of Room 912 and got out a key. I went down there. As I approached, the two in uniform, who had hung back, moved between Fielding and me.

"Mr. Fielding?" I said.

He had his key in the lock, but hadn't turned it yet.

"I can't see anyone now," he said briskly. "I have an urgent appointment."

"It won't take long. It's about a bill for—"

The two bodyguards shifted in a subtle way to block me altogether. They were smooth and cool about it, and they knew exactly what to do.

"Not now," one of them said.

He was dark-haired, with alert dark eyes in a face that would always need a shave. The other one was looser, rangy in build, with yellow sunbleached hair.

The older man had his door open and was going inside.

"No need to fight about it," I said to the dark-faced man. "Either I talk about it now or some judge will decide later."

"Then all right," the guy said. "Beat it."

Mr. Fielding reappeared in the doorway.

"Just a minute, Blick," he said. "What is it about?"

The man called Blick eased back a little, not much. I pulled my documents out of my pocket.

"It's for a shipment of handguns," I said. "Four thousand five hundred dollars."

He looked at the papers but didn't touch them.

"Why hasn't it been paid?" he asked Blick.

"I don't know, sir," Blick said.

"Nick didn't take care of it?"

"I just don't know, Mr. Fielding. There was something about a defect—"

"I believe the receipt carries your own O.K.," I said to Fielding.

I showed it to him.

"Nick didn't take care of it," Fielding said.

He said it slowly and distinctly. He had said it twice now, once in question and once in statement. He had made something clear. Neither of his two henchmen had anything to say.

"I'll have Mrs. Royal draw you a check," Fielding said. "May I have this?"

"Of course."

I gave him the original invoice and kept the rest of the papers.

"If you'll wait a minute," he said, and disappeared.

The door closed. Blick and his friend and I shuffled our feet on the carpet. The door of 910 opened, and Mrs. Edgar Royal looked out at us.

"Roger," she said, "come in, please."

The one with the sunburnt hair headed for the door. A voice sounded behind Mrs. Royal, and she looked over her shoulder and went back inside.

Roger followed her, and the door closed again. Blick, the dark one, stayed with me. As an experiment, I said, "How are you enjoying your stay in Chicago?"

The experiment proved out. He didn't even look at me.

Just come on with the money, Mr. Fielding, I thought.

But thinking doesn't always make it happen. I waited a good long time, alternately looking at Blick and avoiding looking at him. It was hard to see why he felt it necessary to watch over me. I decided he just didn't have any place to go. It was possible he lived in the hotel corridor.

At length Room 910 opened again. Roger came out bearing a check, and Mrs. Royal crooked her finger at Blick, who appeared relieved to get away from me.

"Here's the check," Roger said.

I glanced at the amount, found it correct and nodded to him.

"Thanks," I said.

I walked away down the hall, and when I looked back from the corner, Roger had disappeared. I secured the check in an inner pocket and left the hotel.

* * * *

I had dinner at a German restaurant in the Loop, ate too much and walked around awhile to shake myself down. The stores were closed, and the walking was easy and not unpleasant through the meager crowds. I bought a late paper, glanced through it over a cup of coffee, then went back to the car and headed for Nat Pines' house on the South Side. I pulled up in front of it and turned off the car lights before I remembered my deal with Ed Croft.

That can wait a few minutes, I thought.

Needless to say, Nat was happy to get the money.

"How'd you do it?" he said, while he wrote me a check for $500.

"Gentle persuasion," I said. "I was lucky. I got to the head man."

"He say anything about another order?"

"No," I said. "One thing at a time, Nat."

"Yeah. I'll give him a ring tomorrow."

He offered me a drink, which I declined, and I went out to the car. I had to drive several blocks to find a telephone booth; but it was in use when I got there, and I had to wait five or six minutes. By the time I got to make my call, it was ten thirty.

Good old Ed Croft, I thought.

I found the piece of paper he had given me and called the first number listed. Fifteen rings—no answer. I dialed the second number, and a male voice came on with, "Hello, Duckblind Tavern."

I thought I had a wrong number but gave it a chance.

"Is Karl Schneider there?" I asked him.

"No—" he said, his voice fading as if he were looking over the bar. I was about to hang up when he came on again, saying, "He said if he got any calls he'd be in later."

"O.K., thanks," I said, and hung up.

I looked up the Duckblind Tavern in the classified and found it was on the South Side, though far west of Nat's neighborhood on the South Shore. Still, I thought, it's not so far as it might be, and I promised good old Ed.

I got the car going and drove at a leisurely pace to the vicinity of the Duckblind Tavern. It was clearly an off night. The sizable parking lot was practically empty. I drove into a slot, left the car and strolled to the open door of the joint.

Inside was a small room with a curved bar in one end and some tables and chairs in the other. There were two customers at the bar, a bartender in a red vest behind it and a guy lying face-down, a few degrees off the nearest end, lying stone still with blood around his head. I didn't pay too much heed at first glance. A prostrate man in a bar is not an uncommon sight. But then, having stepped around him, I thought it seemed strange that he was lying face-down. Usually a falling-down drunk falls backward, unless pushed in another direction. Another odd thing—nobody was laughing, and the custom is to get a few laughs out of a far-gone drunk. The two patrons were on their feet to my left, looking down at him, and the bartender had one hand on the wall phone beside his cash register. He took his hand down when I asked him, "What happened?"

"I just called the cops," he said.

I looked at the two customers.

"He was just setting there minding his own business," one of them said, "and these two come in, hauled him off the stool, beat him up and left."

"Took about thirty seconds altogether," the other said.

I squatted beside the bloody head and, without touching it, tried to gauge the damage. There wasn't much to see. The blood had come from a cut over his left eye and from his nose.

"Did you tell the cops to send an ambulance?" I asked the bartender.

He blinked at me over the bar.

"Forgot," he said. "I better call 'em back."

The one on the floor moved suddenly.

"No," he said. "No cops."

He had the bad eye open and looked at me through the blood.

"Take it easy," I said, "you need some help."

He got himself up on an elbow and wiped some of the blood away.

"No cops," he said. "Just get me up and outside. Be all right."

"Listen—" I said.

He moved up higher, trying to get his legs going.

"I'm all right inside," he said. "I'm not busted. Just give me a hand up."

It was a hard choice. If I helped him up and he dropped dead, it would be my doing. But it looked as if he planned to get up anyway, and he could hurt himself trying. I looked at his eyes, and they were fairly clear. I decided his brain was all right.

I braced, leaning over him, and he got one arm over my shoulders. I straightened slowly, and he came up all right. I had to steady him with my hands when he was on his feet. He sagged back against the bar, then moved out from it, still hanging onto me. The bartender stood with his hand on the phone, watching. I shrugged at him.

"Let's go," the guy said. "I got a car out in the parking lot."

"Easy," I said.

He was hanging onto his belly with one hand, and he was good and sick; but he stayed up all right.

"No time for cops," he said. "Help me outside, huh? I'm not wanted."

When I didn't step right along, he tried to pull away from me. He lurched along the bar toward the two bystanders, grabbing at the rail with both hands, and I caught him before he could hit the floor again. I pulled one of his arms over my shoulders and walked him to the door and outside.

"Over there," he said, pointing to the far corner of the lot, near where I had left my own car.

There was no sign of a police car, but I wasn't sure we could make the whole walk before they turned up. From my own selfish point of view, I hoped they would beat us to it. But either it was a busy night, or they had a long way to come, because we got to his car with time to spare.

It was a lightweight sedan, two or three years old, with a downstate license. He put both hands against it, shrugging me off, and worked his way to the front window, as if looking for something.

"Goddam," he said. "The kid—"

"What?"

"The girl. There was a girl with me. Where is she?"

"There wasn't any girl in the bar when I got there," I said.

He stood with one shoulder against the car, and I could see that he was pulling things together inside.

"Got to be found," he said. "Can't be far—"

"If you go back there now," I said, "the cops will be right with you."

"I got to go back."

"All right, I'll take a look for you. What's the girl's name? What does she look like?"

His eyes were working good now, and he used them on me for a full half minute.

"I don't know who you are," he said.

"We're even then," I said.

"My name is Schneider," he said. "Karl Schneider."

I reached for my wallet.

CHAPTER 3

He studied my ID long enough to take it in, and his battered mouth grimaced. I guessed he meant to grin.

"Hello, soul brother," he said. "I'm one, too."

"All right," I said. "Take it easy. I'll go see what I can find on the girl."

I opened the car door and helped him in under the wheel. He rolled the window down, looking out at me.

"Her name is Eloise," he said.

"All right," I said, turning away.

I hadn't got halfway to the bar when a squad car pulled in from the street and stopped near the entrance. The two patrolmen piled out and turned inside without a glance in my direction. I hesitated, then went on, not hurrying. A motor rumbled behind me, and when I looked around, Karl Schneider's car was backing from its slot and heading out of the lot.

The hell with it, I thought.

And then I thought, Go on with it. If you quit now, you'll never know what happened. Besides, there's good old Ed Croft.

I went inside, and apparently the bartender had explained to the cops that everything was all right, the people had all gone away and nobody had died.

"Did you know any of the people in it?" one of the officers asked.

"Well, the guy that got mugged was somebody named Schneider—Karl Schneider. But I didn't know him. He's been hanging around a couple of days; he took a few phone calls here. That's all I know."

"Did he leave here by his own power?"

The two customers who had watched us earlier had now resumed their seats. The bartender hesitated, looked at them and then past the two cops at me.

"I helped him out to his car," I said.

Both the officers looked at me, and one of them asked, "Was this man involved in it?"

"No," the bartender said. "He just helped the guy up."

"At the man's request?"

"That's right," the bartender said.

They came to me.

"Was he getting along all right?" one asked.

"He could walk and he could drive," I said. "I watched him drive away."

I wonder where he went? I thought.

The cops looked at one another and shrugged.

"You want to make a thing?" one of them said to the bartender.

He spread his hands.

"What for?"

"O.K.," the one cop said, and they went out fast.

I gave them time to get their wagon turned around, then ordered a slug of whiskey.

"Did the guy really drive away?" the bartender asked.

"Yeah," I said.

He whistled softly.

"He was hurtin'," he said.

"He said he had a girl with him," I said.

"Uh—yeah, he did."

"You know—he did!" one of the patrons said.

"What happened to her?" I said.

The three of them stared at me and at each other.

"Hey," somebody said.

"I don't know," the bartender said. "She went out."

"Alone?"

He nodded, uncertain.

"Did she hurry?" I said. "Or did she just go out in a leisurely way?"

"She wasn't running," he said.

"I don't know if she went all the way out," one of the customers said. "She went that way. Maybe she went to the ladies' room."

"She probably would be back by now," the bartender said.

"Yeah—unless she was sick or something."

"Is there anybody who could check out the ladies' room for me?" I asked.

The bartender shrugged.

"I told the guy I would see what happened to the girl," I said.

"Well, knock on the door. Couldn't be anybody in there but her."

I went over there, knocked, opened the door and checked out the women's room. Nobody. The two at the bar had their heads together when I headed out of the joint. One of them swung around on his stool.

"I think she left before," he said.

"Before what?"

"Before the thing. That they did to the guy, you know."

"Long before?"

"No, like a minute or something."

"All right, thanks," I said.

There was no sign of Karl Schneider's car in the parking lot, and I felt myself getting away free. I mentally composed a report to Ed Croft: Karl Schneider is some kind of private eye, and he had something to do with a girl named Eloise, who may or may not be connected to the Edgar Royal party—and also to Ray Barnes—and Schneider got himself mussed up in a barroom brawl, and he has disappeared, and that's all I know.

I was climbing smugly into my own car when headlights flashed and Schneider came nosing back in his sedan, not too firmly. He pulled hard right along the wall of the lot, scraped a fender against it and came to a stop. I could see him hunched over the wheel with his head down.

Goddam it, I thought.

While I hesitated, he lifted his head, opened the door and got out of the car. I gave in to my better instincts, crossed the lot and found him making his way around the car to the wall. He had his back against it when I reached him.

"The cops are gone. How are you doing?" I said.

"I saw them leave. Where's the kid, the girl?"

"Not in there. One of the customers said she left a minute before they mugged you."

He put both hands on his face and pulled them down slowly, drawing his eyelids down and letting them snap shut.

"You're not well," I said. "You ought to get in a sack somewhere."

"No."

"Where's your place? Or are you just passing through?"

"No, we got a place down the street, by the day. We got to get to California, if I can move her."

"I'll help you over to your place. Probably that's where the girl went, waiting for you."

"No."

"Then she'll turn up in the morning."

He pushed himself up against the wall and raised his face, staring at me in the half-dark.

"Who in the hell are you?" he said.

"I told you."

"Tell me again."

You've got to have plenty of credentials to be a good guy.

I got out my wallet again and let him look at the ID. "Oh, yeah," he said. "I remember."

"If I check out clean enough for you," I said, "could we go now? I'll give you a lift, or follow, whatever you want."

He was gazing past me toward the open door of the tavern.

"I promise," I said, "she wasn't there."

"Her name is Eloise," he said. "She's Nick Royal's daughter. She's a half-nutty kid. Anything can happen to her. Anything."

* * * *

I guess we stood by that wall for about five minutes, just stood there, him looking at that tavern door, or around at different things; me waiting for him to get up enough juice to move. At one point I walked over and turned off his car lights. On the floor under the wheel was an imitation derringer in a worn leather holster. I pushed it back under the seat, out of sight. When I got back, he was where I had left him.

"If it's like that with the girl," I said, "those cops were the best friends you ever had."

"No, you don't understand," he said.

"All right," I said.

I was getting tired of him and tired of standing around.

"Because her daddy's in trouble," he said. "Bad trouble."

I restrained an impulse to hit him in the mouth. At about that moment, he turned suddenly and got sick to his stomach, holding himself with one hand against the wall, leaning far out. When he finished unloading, he bent double, hanging onto himself in the middle with both hands, and he would have fallen over if I hadn't straightened him up enough to get him against the wall.

"Come on, you're sick," I said. "I'll take you to a hospital. You can think better—"

He pushed at me with one hand.

"I'm all right now," he said. "Listen—" He had his hand in his pants pocket. "I remember you now, I mean who you are. Listen, I need some help. Will you hang around?"

"Naturally I'll help you get where you have to go," I said.

"I don't mean just for now. I'm buying some of your real time."

He had two $50 bills in his hand, sticking them at me.

"Put the money away," I said.

"Come on, for Christ's sake! I'm one too. But right now I need help."

"O.K., brother," I said, "but I don't have more than fifty dollars' worth of time available."

I took one of the fifties and pushed the other one back at him.

"Now let's go," I said. "Your car or mine?"

"If you don't mind," he said.

We went over to my car. He walked along all right now and he didn't need any help getting in, once he got the door open. That took two tries.

"Where?" I said.

"Down the street here, first signal turn right, one block and left, about half a block."

I got it started, driving carefully so as not to jar him. I was developing uneasy feelings about Karl Schneider. All right, if he was a private eye. But we come in a variety of cloaks, and sometimes the daggers are bloody. I didn't like the rub of the fifty against my pocket lining. I could give it back to him, I thought, once he got through the trauma. I could refer him to somebody if he really needed help. Then I could go home to bed. With any luck I could stay in bed twelve or thirteen hours.

Selfish? You bet your sweet—

"I'm from downstate—Springfield," he said. "I used to be with an agency there, but I went on my own."

"Uh-huh," I said. "How are things?"

"You can see how things are."

"There's always a way out."

"Not out of this."

I made the first turn, and he said, "I'm tied to this one with blood."

My feelings went from bad to worse.

"What about this Nick Royal?" I asked.

After a while he said, "I'll tell you about him. But we got to find the girl first. The girl is more important."

"Why?"

"She's a girl. And she's younger."

I made the left turn, and drove about half a block. He stopped me in front of an apartment hotel called the Venetian Arms. The main entrance door was open, but the lobby facilities were closed tight and a sign on the desk read no vacancy. There was a nightbell below a card reading manager. I got into an elevator with Karl Schneider, and we started grinding our way upward.

"The two that mugged you," I said. "Did you get a look at them?"

"No, hell, no. It was too fast. They came from behind me."

"Is there any chance they might have snatched the girl?" I asked.

He looked at me, blinking with his bad eye.

"I try not to think about that."

"I got one more," I said. "Who is Ray Barnes?"

He mumbled some obscenities and wiped his mouth with his hand.

"He's a goddam psychology professor at the state college. The kid—Eloise—is hung on him."

The cage stopped with a lurch at the eleventh floor. We got out of it, walked a narrow carpeted hall, past four rooms, and stopped at 1119. He fished in his pocket, found a key and unlocked the door. It was dead quiet in the hall and I could hear him breathe, a little too fast, wheezing faintly.

The apartment was lighted. I walked ahead of Schneider into a cramped vestibule with a coat closet on one side and a solid unadorned wall on the other. Dead ahead, across the square living room, a large man in an expensive white sport shirt was seated on a davenport.

He didn't move. He didn't speak. He had black curly hair on a big round head, and black eyes in a smooth pale face. The eyes didn't move any more than the rest of him, as I stopped to let Karl Schneider pass me.

"Hello, Nick," Schneider said.

The big one just sat there, gazing at Schneider, not even blinking. After a long time, his eyes shifted and began to gaze at me.

"This is a surprise," Schneider said.

The one he had called Nick opened his mouth enough to let some words out.

"Where's Eloise?" he said.

"Tell you what happened—" Schneider said.

"No," Royal said, "don't tell me. Just take me where she is."

He began to get up on his feet. It took some time because he stood tall. I judged his height at 6 feet, 7 or 8 inches, and his weight at about 280. A lot of it was in his shoulders and upper torso.

"All right," Schneider said, "just take it easy."

Several things happened at once—an instant bad scene. Nick Royal's eyes widened and shifted. Schneider fell away to my right, and within a watch tick a blast in the back of my head drove me down into a black void. Mercifully, the one blow was enough to do the job. I was spared lingering pangs—or if there were pangs, I was too unconscious to notice.

CHAPTER 4

The crudest phase of coming around after a head blow is the mixed-up scene behind your eyes. You make things out vaguely, but it takes concentration to learn what they are. And concentration makes the head pains worse, so you try to avoid it. But at the same time you're worried you might get hit again and you have to find out what your situation is. So you concentrate anyway, and the pain gets worse, but you hang in with it, and little by little your eyes get to working and you can see what you've been trying to find.

The first recognizable thing I saw was a knife. It was a fake antique switchblade knife, half hilt and half blade, the kind that when you press a button, the blade shoots straight out from the hilt. Altogether, it measured about ten inches. There was blood on the blade, and the thing was lying on the rug about two inches from the limp fingers of my right hand. The sight of it caused my stomach to cramp and my eyes to squeeze shut. I didn't want to see anything else. But after about a minute my brain shifted to a higher gear, and I looked again. Not only was there blood on the knife, there was blood on my hand and fingers.

Get out of here, the brain said.

It was my most productive thought so far, and I started to lever myself up on my elbows, holding the hand with the blood on it far out to avoid smearing myself elsewhere. Then I tried to roll on my side and gather my legs up, but they had gone to sleep. I could tell by the futile straining in my thighs that my lower legs wouldn't move. It scared me badly, and my heart began pounding like a fast-moving wheel with a flat tire on it. I got up on the elbows, looked down that way and saw the rest of the bad real dream: a big guy in a white sport shirt lying facedown across my legs. But not so completely facedown as to hide the red smear on the front of the white shirt. Happily, the face was turned away from me. The back of his head looked posthumous.

Nick Royal, I thought.

There were sounds of heavy footsteps, and the door thudded lightly, then opened, somewhere behind and beyond my head. I knew the door had opened by the sudden draft. And next there were two guys in more or less baggy suits looking down at me. And at Mr. Royal.

The first words spoken were, "Find the phone and call in."

They were spoken by the one who stood on my right, his shoe almost touching the bloody knife. He took another look at me, then he looked at the knife, then he leaned over, far over, not moving his feet, and picked up the nearer of Nick Royal's wrists. He held onto it for about half a minute, then dropped it. It fell on the carpet heavily. I could hear the other one speaking to the phone, but I couldn't tell exactly where he was. The pain in the back of my head was enhanced by my strained position. I looked up at the guy and said, "Will you help me up, please?"

"In a minute," he said. "Soon as my partner gets back."

"My name—" I said.

"All right," he said. "In a minute."

The other one came back, and the first one said, "We got to get this one up. I don't want to move that body any more than necessary. Try to ease it up far enough to get his legs out."

The other guy, the younger one, got hold of Nick Royal's belt with both hands and pulled up.

"Jesus," he said through his teeth.

I managed to pull one numb leg free, but the other was still pinned and the cop lifted the body a little higher. I got the leg out from under and started to roll away from the cop in order to get up, and the one holding the body let it down gently, while the other one put his hands under my arms, ostensibly to help me, but actually to check me out for weapons. I didn't have any on me.

When I stood on my feet, my lower legs filled with hot needles. I made myself stay on them, then walked across the room and sat down on the davenport with my head in my hands. I had forgotten about the blood, and when I felt it, still sticky, against my face, I jerked my hand away and nearly fell over. Then I held the palm up on my knee and stared at it. The older cop had a notebook out.

"Let's hear about it," he said. "You said your name was—"

I reached inside my jacket with my clean hand and pulled out my wallet. The younger cop took it and read my name from the ID, and the other one wrote in the notebook.

"All right," he said. "Tell us what happened."

"Like this—" I said. Then I said, "Wait a minute. Don't you have a little speech to make first?"

He scratched at his temple with a stubby pencil and gazed at me.

"Thanks for reminding me," he said. And then, very fast: "Have right to call a lawyer…anything you say may be used against you, is that all right?"

"That's fine," I said. "I don't need a lawyer. This is what happened. A guy got beat up in a bar. I helped him up and outside, and after a while I brought him over here, where he said he was living, and we came in the apartment here, and this one on the floor was sitting where I am now, and he said, 'Where's Eloise?' and he got up and headed toward me, and something hit me on the back of the head. I came to about five minutes ago. And that's all I know."

The two of them looked at each other. The one with the pencil didn't write anything down.

"You can check out about the thing in the bar," I said, "because the bartender called the police, and two of them came, and they'll have a report on it."

"What was the name of the bar?"

"The Duckblind Tavern, over on Eighty-first."

Still he didn't write anything down, and it was beginning to bug me.

"What was the fella's name?" he said.

"Which one?"

"The one you said brought you up here?"

"Schneider—Karl Schneider—he claimed. But I don't believe him much. He said he was a private eye from downstate, but I don't believe that either."

"Who beat him up?"

"Two guys. I don't know who."

"Do you know the name of this one?"

"Schneider called him Nick. I believe his full name is Nick Royal."

There was a sport jacket, about size 44, hanging on the back of a straight chair, and the younger cop went to it, felt inside and came out with a wallet. He flipped it open and took it to the other one.

"Nick Royal," he said. "California driver's license."

"Schneider said Royal was in bad trouble," I said.

"You believed that?" the cop said.

"I wouldn't argue with a dead man," I said.

"Better call in the name," the cop said, and the younger one went to the phone again. Now I saw it was on a table against the wall just inside the main room. In the vestibule, the coat closet door was ajar, and I saw a woman's topcoat hanging in it.

"Who is Eloise?" the cop asked me.

"I don't know. Schneider said she was Royal's daughter."

I was feeling pretty good about the coat being in the closet and about the fact that they could check part of my story at the bar. But the blood on my hand and face was bothering me. I could smell it now, coppery and acrid.

"Would it be all right if I wash up now?" I asked.

The cop seemed to think it over.

"In a minute," he said.

What he meant was, after the crew gets here and gets samples of it.

"What kind of trouble was Royal supposed to be in?" the cop asked.

"Schneider didn't say. He said he had to get the girl to California."

"You saw the girl?"

"No, never," I said.

The younger one came back from the phone.

"Royal has no record here," he said. "This one"—he nodded toward me—"checks out clear."

The cop with the pencil looked at me.

"He does, huh?"

The younger one looked at the mess on the floor and shrugged. I wondered who would arrive to take charge of the investigation. I seemed to remember that Donovan was off duty for a couple of days.

A woman wearing a dressing gown and large pink hair curlers looked into the room.

"What's going on in here?" she asked.

The older cop turned his head to look at her and said, "We're officers, ma'am. Are you the manager?"

"Yes, I am. I'm Mrs. Brody."

"Did you hear any disturbance tonight?"

"No," she said. "Not a thing."

From where she stood, she couldn't see Royal's body. She looked at me with deep suspicion.

"Did you have a guest registered in this apartment?" the cop asked.

"Two guests—a man named Schneider and his, uh, niece he said she was."

"You didn't believe him?"

"In this business—" she said.

"Well, Mrs. Brody, I'm sorry to have to tell you, there's been a homicide here and I'd like to come talk to you pretty soon, if you don't mind getting dressed. What is your apartment number?"

"First floor, apartment twenty—what did you say?"

"I said there's been a homicide—"

"You mean murder?"

"That's approximately what I mean," he said.

"Oh, my God," she said.

She lingered a moment, trying to see the evidence, then turned and disappeared.

I had begun to think things over, and when you think things over, you raise questions.

How did Royal get in here, I wondered, if his visit was a surprise, unless somebody let him in? How did he know where to come if Schneider was just checked in for a couple of days en route to California? Schneider may have known he was here and was putting me on when he seemed to be surprised. Schneider may even have given him a key. Or Eloise may have let him in.

Where is Eloise? I thought.

"Can you give me a description of this girl—Eloise?" the cop asked me.

"I never saw her," I said.

"You say you got hit in the back of the head. You hear anybody coming?"

"No."

"Was it Schneider?"

"It couldn't have been Schneider, he was in front of me. But it could have been Schneider that put the knife in Royal."

The hell with you, Schneider, I thought.

"You know for sure somebody put a knife in him?"

"Well, no, naturally not."

And then I remembered something.

"Only thing is," I said, "Schneider didn't have a knife on him."

"You frisked him?"

"Not on purpose. But I had to help him, grab him a few times, and unless he had it strapped inside his leg or somewhere like that, I'm sure he wasn't carrying it."

Sirens sounded down the street.

Let it be Donovan, I thought.

It won't be Donovan, I thought. This is bad-luck night. Never help a stranger.

The sirens stopped. I looked at my watch, and it read two fifteen. The blood was drying rapidly now, drawing at the skin of my hand and face.

Goddam it, I thought.

But maybe, if not Donovan, it will be somebody I know. I know quite a few of the fellows.

"Will you tell me something?" I asked the cop with the notebook. "How did you happen to come up here?"

He brooded at me and scratched his head with his pencil.

"We got a call," he said.

"From Karl Schneider?"

"No," he said. He looked away, then back at me. "It was a woman's voice," he said.

I could hear them coming now, in the hall, the tread quick and syncopated.

CHAPTER 5

The lieutenant in charge was not Donovan. His name was Joe Preston, and I had a nodding acquaintance with him, that was all. He was younger than Donovan, and he had a long way to go to the top, which was where he planned to get, and he had a very professional attitude. This was good for him and his plans, but it wasn't awfully helpful to me.

His professionalism extended to the point where he ignored me for the first ten minutes. Good psychological tactics. He had a bad scene to cope with and a staff to marshal, and that's what he took care of first. I sat there contemplating my bloody hand and felt left out of things—a ridiculous feeling, considering how all the way in I was.

Lieutenant Preston did get around to me eventually. In an admirably formal way, he asked permission to collect a specimen of the blood on my hand.

"Sure," I said.

A lab guy with a spatula carefully scraped some off my hand into a sterile envelope. When he had enough, he looked at my face.

"It's all from the same batch," I said.

He took my word for it and went away. A photographer was shooting the scene from various angles. He had the old-fashioned, outsized flashbulbs, and every shot was like a slap at the backs of my eyeballs. My brain felt inside out.

"May I wash up now?" I asked Preston.

"All right," he said. "You know where the bathroom is?"

"No," I said. "I don't know anything at all. Only that I came in over there and got smacked in the head, and when I woke up I couldn't move, and then your men started arriving."

He looked at me without expression, then nodded backward, and we found the bathroom. He stood in the doorway while I washed my face and hands and applied some cold water to the lump on my head.

"How long did you know this Nick Royal?" he asked.

"About two minutes. Come to think of it, I never really met him. Nobody introduced us."

"You've been framed, huh?"

"Yes. Exactly."

"All by accident—guy picks you up—spur-of-the-moment—sets up a frame—no contact with anybody else—just happened. Like rain or something."

He had a good strong point, and I could feel the tile floor under me turning to mud. Schneider couldn't have expected me to turn up, and he'd had no real chance to set up a thing. If Schneider was the one who did the killing, it was an impromptu frame-up. But it couldn't have been Schneider alone. Some actual person had given me the headache.

"I know how it looks," I said. "But it's true. If Schneider did it to Royal, I happened to be a lucky bystander."

"But you told Sergeant Keynes it couldn't have been Schneider that cold-conked you."

"All right, there was somebody else. He could have been in the coat closet. The closet door was closed when we came in, and I noticed it was open after I woke up. Or somebody could have been watching from another apartment."

"How would he know what to watch for—if Schneider didn't tip him in advance?"

Preston was at least giving me the break of open controversy. If my own logic broke down, whose fault was it?

"Maybe he was just watching for Schneider. At least two men had their eyes on Schneider somewhere along the line. Two of them beat him up in that bar."

"Let's get out of here," Preston said.

I followed him into the living room, where the lab men were working around the body. A man from the coroner's office was on his knees, writing on forms. Two assistants stood around with a folding stretcher, waiting. The photographer was still there, but he wasn't taking any pictures.

"Wait here," Preston told me.

He crossed to where Sergeant Keynes and his partner were standing in the vestibule. They went into a five-minute conference, and I stood on one foot or another and wished the pain in my head would diminish.

Preston crooked his finger at me, and I went over there. The three of them made a short study of me. Then Preston said, "You're in a bad fix here. All you've got going for you is that you have a lump on your head—in the back—and you've been cooperative. I'm not going to hold you now. But don't leave town. We'll check out the Duckblind incident as soon as we can find the witnesses, and we're looking for Schneider. Go home and get some sleep. You may need it."

"O.K., Lieutenant," I said. "Thanks for the break."

"Don't thank me. If you had anything on your record—anything at all—"

"I know."

"That's all for now."

I pushed past Sergeant Keynes and got into the hall. A small cluster of people in various stages of undress was gathered some distance from the door. They wanted to see what was going on, but nobody wanted to take the initiative. They moved to let me pass, and nobody asked me any questions. I was glad I had been able to wash my face.

Just beyond the group, standing alone against the wall, was a girl about seventeen or eighteen, wearing a sweater and a miniskirt over white fishnet stockings. Her hair was long and thick, enclosing her face on both sides and down to her eyebrows in front. She looked like a full-grown girl with a miniature face. It was neither pretty nor homely, just very small-looking, with a short, sharp little nose and a pale, narrow mouth. I passed her, heading for the elevator, and when I got there she had contrived to join me. I pushed the button, the cage opened, and she got in with me. We got two floors down and she said, "Is your name Mac?"

"Yes," I said. "You are Eloise?"

"Uh-huh."

"How did you know me?"

"I didn't know really. I took a chance."

"How did you know there was such a person as me?"

"Karl Schneider told me."

"Recently?"

"A while ago."

"Where is Karl Schneider now?"

"I don't know. He called me on the phone."

My hands were sticky, and I looked at my right palm where the blood had been.

"Do you know what happened in that apartment up there?" I asked her.

"Yes. My father died in it."

I looked at her little face.

Cool, I thought. So goddam cool.

"Did Karl Schneider tell you that, too?"

"No," she said. "I went in there, and I saw him—and you."

"I see. So it was you who called the police."

"Yes."

"Where were you when the police arrived?"

"I was… hiding, around the corner up there in the hall."

"Do you know who killed your father?"

There was some pause. The elevator reached the first floor and stopped with a jolt.

"It wasn't you?" she said.

"No, it wasn't me."

"Then I don't know."

I looked into her bright dark-blue eyes, framed in all that hair, and the back of my head throbbed steadily.

"I think you and I had better go somewhere and talk about things," I said.

"I guess so," she said.

We left the elevator and walked past the closed office and outside. She was about as high as my biceps. She came along without protest, silent, with a gliding stride like that of a dancer. I was a little put out with her but couldn't figure out whether it was because of her association with Schneider or merely that she had taken me by surprise. As I helped her into the car, I asked, "You didn't identify yourself when you called the police?"

"No," she said. "It didn't seem very real."

I put a hand gingerly on the back of my head.

"It was real," I said.

"But not really real."

I got the car going.

"Why did you run out on Karl Schneider in the bar, when he was attacked?" I asked her.

"I don't know. There wasn't anything I could do about it. I was afraid they'd do something to me, too."

Fairly good sense, I thought grudgingly.

"Did you recognize the two men, the ones who beat him up?"

A substantial pause.

"No, I didn't," she said.

I didn't believe her.

"You say you don't know where Schneider is now?"

"I don't know. He said he was calling from a pay phone."

"How did he know where to call you?"

No answer.

I made the turn at the signal light and drove west toward the Duckblind Tavern. It was still open, but there were no cars in the parking lot, none at all, especially not Schneider's. I hadn't expected it to be there, but you have a way of hoping.

"He called me at that all-night coffee shop back there," she said.

"Back where?"

I couldn't remember an all-night coffee shop in the vicinity. I drove about half a mile down the main street and paused at a major intersection. Eloise pointed to our left.

"Down there," she said.

I turned, drove about two blocks and, sure enough, there was a small coffee shop still doing business at 3:18 in the a.m.

"We'll get some coffee," I said.

"Can't I just wait—"

"No," I said. "I'm responsible for you whether I want to be or not, and you'll have to come along."

"You're pretty bossy, huh?"

"Only with women and children," I said. "Let's go."

I helped her out, and we went into the place. It was one of the real old-timers, with a cafeteria service at the back, one-armed chairs along the walls and white-topped tables down the middle. There were half a dozen customers, all male, but Karl Schneider was not among them. We went to the counter and ordered coffee.

"Hungry?" I asked her.

"No," she said.

Her face was closed and sullen now. I regretted it, but my head hurt and I couldn't be altogether nice. I took the coffee to a table, and she sat down across from me, holding her cup in both small hands, sniffing at it.

"When Schneider called you," I said, "what did he want you to do?"

She shrugged.

"He must have had some suggestions," I said. "Something besides the information that I was close at hand. I was in dreamland and he must have known it."

"He said—Well, he just said to stay here and he would come and get me."

"How long did you stay?"

"I sat here a long time—at least half an hour—and I couldn't just sit here forever. So I went back to the apartment to see if he was there."

"What did he tell you had happened over there?"

"He just said there had been some trouble. He said if he didn't make it over here—to the coffee shop—I should look up a man named Mac."

"What I'm trying to get at," I said, "is how you figured it out to look me up in that apartment, if Schneider didn't tell you I was there."

Her tiny face twisted with impatience.

"Like this," she said. "I sat here, and Karl didn't come. I went back to the apartment, and I had a key and I went in, and my father was on the floor there, and I knew he was dead just by looking at him, and I thought you were dead, too, and I called the police—"

"From the apartment?"

"Yes, that's where the phone was. And I was going to wait for the police; but I couldn't stand it in there, because it wasn't real or anything, and I went down the hall and waited."

"All right so far," I said. "Now, how did you happen to guess that I—the guy in the apartment with your father—was the Mac you were supposed to look up?"

Her lips made a spitting gesture, and she shook her head hard, causing the long hair to whip around her taut, strained little face.

"I don't know. I guess Jesus told me."

I drank some coffee.

"Schneider told you, didn't he?" I said. "He told you I was up there. Did he tell you I killed your father?"

"No! He didn't tell me that. He told me not to tell you—"

"He told you I was there and he probably said something like, 'Don't ever tell him I told you this.'"

"Well, he—"

But why, I thought, did he also tell her to look me up?

On a wall shelf near the front door was a telephone in a plastic shell.

"Please stay here a minute," I said.

I went to the phone, dialed the Palmer House and a clerk came on. I asked for Ed Croft, and there was an extended pause.

"I'm sorry, sir, Mr. Croft is busy at the moment—"

"It's very urgent," I said.

"Well, just a moment."

After quite a while he came back.

"May I ask who's calling?" he said.

A small, belated bell clanged in my mind.

"Mr. Croft is with the police?" I asked.

Another pause, then reluctantly, "Yes, sir."

"I'm reporting to him on a related matter," I said. "It could mean quite a lot to the hotel."

"Just a minute, I'll see what I can do."

While I waited, I watched Eloise at the table. She sat slumped in her chair, looking sullen and furtive. I decided she had a right to look furtive.

Ed Croft came on the line, his voice gruff and hurried. "Yeah?"

"Mac," I said. "The cops are there?"

"Uh-huh. Something happened to a guy named Royal Nick—"

"I know. Are they talking to Mrs. Royal now?"

"And the others."

"Is Karl Schneider there?"

"No. Schneider? No."

"All right, listen. He's mixed up in it. I'm out on the South Side with Mrs. Royal's daughter—"

"With who?"

"Eloise, her daughter. Nick Royal's daughter."

"She's married to *Edgar* Royal."

"I don't know about that. Listen, that guy Ray Barnes—is he still in the hotel?"

"I guess so. I haven't—"

"He's not with the cops?"

"No."

"Try to keep your eye on him. I'll check in later."

"Wait, Mac, will you—"

"No time now. I'll call you again."

I hung up and went back to the table. Eloise stirred as if ready to move on.

"We'll go in a minute," I said. "Try to finish your coffee."

"I don't like coffee."

"I'll get you something else."

"No, let's just get out of here."

"In a minute. Do you know a man named Ray Barnes?"

Her eyes turned into triangles, squashed shut, then slowly opened and rounded.

"What if I do?" she said.

"It's important."

"It's important to me all right."

"What is he to you?"

"He's my—boyfriend!"

She said it with sudden intensity, as if it had just occurred to her and she had to prove it in the same breath.

"All right then," I said. "You know he's at the Palmer House."

"I know that's where he's supposed to be."

"And your mother—she's there, too."

"Well—not with him, I mean—"

"I know that. The thing is, the police are at the hotel, talking to your mother, and to Edgar Royal and Mr. Fielding, and maybe some others—"

"Edgar Royal is my uncle," she said.

"O.K."

"My mother divorced my father and married my uncle."

"I see."

She shrugged.

"It's all right with me. I don't give a shit."

"I'm sure I don't either. The point I'm trying to reach is: What am I going to do about you?"

"What do you mean do about me? You don't have to do anything about me. Just let me get the hell out of this crummy place—"

"We'll get out of here. I'll take you to the hotel, to your mother."

We got all the way to the car, and I had the motor running before she said, "No, not my mother. Take me to Ray Barnes."

"How old are you?" I asked.

"Seventeen," she said.

"Then you don't have much to say about it."

"I do, too! I'm of age!"

"Not in Chicago."

Suddenly she was on her knees on the seat, banging on the back of it with her little fists, screaming at me. I pulled into the curb.

"You take me to Ray Barnes, or let me out," she said. "I can get there myself. I've got money."

I drew back to stay in the clear. The shape I was in, if she should hit me in the head I'd pass out.

"Listen to my problem," I said. "I don't know Ray Barnes. I've met your mother. You're under age. If I take you to her, I'm in the clear."

"You—fink!" she said.

"Okay, I'm a fink, but I'd rather be a clean fink than a dirty knight—in some jail."

She had stopped with the fists, and I decided it was safe to get moving again. She slumped in the corner of the seat and put her face in her hands.

"You can call the police and enter a complaint," I said, "after we get to the hotel. How's that?"

She just sat there, huddled, saying bad words. Nothing unusual about that, the way things go nowadays, but she spoke them without conviction, though not without heat. It had the effect of monkey talk out of her miniature face. I guess it began to sound like that to her, too, because finally she stopped. We were approaching the Loop from the west when she began to speak in a moderate, little-girl voice.

"I'm not supposed to tell anyone yet, but I guess I have to tell you. My father didn't want me to go back to my mother, if anything happened to him, I mean. He wanted me to stay here and finish school and he wanted Karl Schneider to be my—kind of take care of me."

Your father must have been out of his mind, I thought. "What about this Ray Barnes?" I said.

"My father didn't know anything about Ray Barnes."

"But your father knew Schneider?"

"He knew him a long time ago, in the war."

"It may be true that that was your father's wish," I said. "But you're old enough to make your own decisions—legally—some of them."

"I've already told you about that."

"I've told you my problem, too," I said.

"Yes, but you don't have to stay there. You can just go away and forget it."

She had me there. The rest of it I could believe or not, but she had a good point now.

"Karl Schneider was going to take me to California to see my father," she said, "and we came up here to Chicago because Ray Barnes was here and I had to see him."

"What does Karl Schneider think of Ray Barnes?"

"He hates him."

"Then why would he agree to bring you to Chicago to see him?"

"Because I love him—Ray Barnes, I mean. And also because if he hadn't agreed to bring me here, I wouldn't have agreed to go to California with him."

A heavy pain thrust in my head, and I wished I could get my hands on Karl Schneider, if only for a couple of minutes.

We were coming into Wells Street on Congress. The lights ahead were yellow and red and orange. There were some other colors mixed in that must have formed in my poor head exclusively.

"All I'm asking for," Eloise said, "is a break, one little break, to call up the man I love."

It didn't sound so odd, coming from her. Still—

You're too young to lean on love, I thought.

I would live to learn.

I turned north on Wells and headed for the river. On the Near North Side, I turned east on Chicago, and my own sweet home was only blocks away. It felt good, but I was undecided about the girl. If I let her make telephone calls, she would have to let me in on them, and that could be some trick to turn.

I got onto my own street from Michigan and found a place to park half a block past my office toward the lake. I helped Eloise out of the car, and we started back up the street.

"Where are we?" she said.

"My place," I said. "The office is in front and I live in the back."

"It's old here," she said.

"Yes, that it is."

Across the street, a car parked near the entrance to Tony's bar caught my eye. I had seen it before. There was a guy sitting in it behind the wheel, and he looked even more familiar than the car. I put my hand on Eloise's arm and she stopped.

"Let's go over there a minute," I said.

"Well—"

"Come on," I said.

I led her into the street and up to within about six feet of the open front window of the parked car. Karl Schneider looked out at us.

CHAPTER 6

In the bad light, with what had happened to his face, he looked like a gargoyle. His mouth moved stiffly.

"You found her," he said. Then, looking at her, "How are you, kid?"

"Don't call me kid," she said.

"O.K."

He looked at me again.

"Explanation time," I said. "You want to get out of there on your own, or shall I pull you out?"

He grinned, in a way.

"I guess you could," he said. "I'll get out. Could we go in there and have a drink?"

Tony's would be open for another hour and a half, and it wouldn't be crowded. For another thing, surely, there would be aspirin in there.

"I don't want to go in there," Eloise said.

"You'll have to for now," I said. "Mr. Schneider and I have some talking to do."

Except that I had caught up with Schneider, it had been a bad choice to give Eloise her little break. I needed nothing as much as to get her off my hands.

Schneider was getting out of the car. I started to lead Eloise around the back end of it toward Tony's; then I stopped when a police car pulled up, double-parked, in front of my office. The driver got out, and a moment later a woman left the car. Both were in plain clothes. They headed up the steps to my office.

"Let's get out of the goddam street," Schneider said.

"Cop-shy?" I said.

"For now I am," he said. "I got a lot to do."

"Well," I said, "I'm too hot to play games with them. Take Eloise in the joint, and I'll see what they want."

I had a pretty good idea what a male-female officer detail would want, but I had to hear it from them.

At Tony's door, I said, "Don't run out with her, Schneider, or I'll turn you in if it takes, on my own time, till Christmas."

"I know it," he said.

They went inside, and I crossed the street. I met the two of them coming back from my office steps. The male cop had papers in his hand.

"Looking for me?" I asked him.

"Who are you?" he said.

I told him.

"Yes."

He hauled out his ID, flashed it and said, "You know the whereabouts of a young lady named Eloise Royal, age seventeen, daughter of Gretchen and Nick Royal?"

"I probably do," I said. "What's the thing?"

"We have an order to return her to the custody of her mother, Room Nine Ten, Palmer House."

It all seemed to check out.

"She says she doesn't want to go there," I said.

"I'm afraid she doesn't have a choice right now," the guy said. "She can take legal action later."

"All right," I said. "She's over at Tony's. Will you give me a couple of minutes to fill her in? She's in kind of a state."

They looked at each other, and the guy nodded. The three of us crossed over to Tony's, and they stood near the door.

"Not more than two minutes," the guy said, "or we'll have to come in."

I nodded and went inside. There was a bartender, one customer asleep with his head on the bar, and Schneider and Eloise were sitting in the last booth along the wall. I went down there.

"Juvenile cops," I said. "They're picking up Eloise."

"What for?" Schneider said.

"To take her to her mother."

He shook his head.

"Her father didn't want her to go back there."

"Her father is dead," I said.

Eloise sat across from Schneider, looking straight ahead.

"No choice," I said. "They gave me two minutes, then they'll be in. They've got valid papers."

Schneider was stuck good, and he knew it. He got up from the booth, watching Eloise.

"Go ahead with them, kid," he said. "I'll find a way to help you. Believe me."

She just gazed straight ahead. Schneider walked back toward the men's room and disappeared.

"I won't go," Eloise said.

"Yes you will," I said. "You can't fight them. Play it cool. Do the fighting later, on your own ground."

"If Ray Barnes was here—"

"It will be easier to get hold of Ray Barnes at the Palmer House than from out here," I said.

There was a moment of sheer, glum silence.

"Here they come," the bartender said quietly.

He was leaning against the backbar with his arms folded. We had known each other a long time.

"Up we go," I said. "Be a big girl now. They won't eat you."

The two officers had come in and were approaching the bar. I touched Eloise's arm. She pulled it away, slid out of the booth and slapped her skirt into place.

"Eloise Royal?" the male officer said.

"Yes, that's me," she said.

The policewoman was about forty-two and had no doubt gone through this scene eight hundred and sixty-two times before. She took over without really appearing to take over.

"Come on, dear," she said, "we'll take you to your hotel. It's late."

"I'm not sleepy," Eloise said.

"I know, honey," the lady cop said, "but I am."

Eloise gave her a hard look, then surrendered and went along. Neither of them touched her. I tapped the male officer on the shoulder, and he turned back.

"How did you know to come to me?" I asked.

"I'm not sure," he said. "I just got the order from the desk."

"O.K., thanks," I said. "Hang in, Eloise. Everything will turn out all right."

She didn't look back. I went to the bar and asked Bill the bartender for a couple of aspirin and a slug of whiskey. If one didn't work, the other might.

I was sitting in the booth, working on the slug, when Schneider came back. He stood around for a minute, then sat down across from me and drank his half-finished highball.

"The girl is nothing to me," I said. "She has a mother. Nick Royal was nothing to me. You are nothing to me. I live in this town. I have to live a certain way. That's my story. What about yours?"

His beat-up face hung over the highball glass like a ravaged moon. His mouth cracked in that grin he sometimes wore. I felt like the inside of a movie with Bogey in it.

"Nick Royal was my colonel," he said, "in the Pacific, the old South Pacific. He was a real Marine. I was only stuck there. I was his sergeant."

I stared at him.

"If this is one of those heart stories—" I said.

He ignored me.

"We got along good, though. He didn't care if I wasn't a real Marine. I won't bore you with the distinction between a real Marine and the others—"

"Thank you," I said.

"Anyway, I'd been lucky, I never got in a real bad place until one day, on…one of those islands…we were only a couple of hours off the beach, and a few of us up front got detached and then lost, and we were in a mess. So when it got hairy that way, it was pretty much every man for himself, and the group began to break up, some getting hit and others heading out one way or another, trying to get back to the outfit. And then I got hit. I never saw where it came from; but it was in the legs and the back, and I was flat.

"When I came around, one of the guys was there, stretched out on the ground, his eyes moving all the time, ready to blast anything that moved. 'You hit?' he said, and I said, 'Yeah,' and he said, 'Can you walk?' and I tried, but I couldn't even get my legs bent, let alone stand on 'em. 'We'd never make it piggyback,' he said. 'There's Japs everywhere you look here. But I think I know where the outfit is now, and maybe I can get to it. I'll tell 'em where you are.' Then he checked my guns and left me some ammo and some extra water, and he took off.

"I'd been hit in the morning and I laid there all day. There was kind of a pile of rocks and a lot of brush, but nowhere to really hole up that I could see. I kept passing out and coming to, and every time I came to, it was a big surprise to me. I could hear stuff going on, sometimes real close, but I never did see anybody. By the time the sun went down, I was half out of my mind, and I tried to get up again and passed out, and the next time I came to it was dark. And there wasn't anything much going on anymore, except from a distance, and that would have been off the ships over the-beachhead. I could hear 'em blast off, and later I could hear 'em drop somewhere. Once in a while there were flares close by. I couldn't understand how I was still alive. I drank the rest of the water I had and let myself go, figuring that would be the last time. And then I woke up once more, and there was a flash beam in my face. I had my sidepiece in my hand, and I aimed it straight at the light, and a voice said, 'Knock it off, Sergeant, it's your colonel—Nick.'

"So then he told me what the situation was, which was very bad. He had the guy with him that had left me before, who had made it all right back to the outfit, and Nick Royal had just happened to be there when he told the captain about me. I got this later. When Nick heard it, he said, 'Where is he?' And the guy tried to tell him, and Nick said, 'Could you find your way back there?' and the guy said sure, and Nick said, 'All right, let's go.' You see, it wasn't really very far, in distance. But it was that bad mess all around.

"Anyway, they found the place. 'We'll have to make it before daylight,' Nick said, 'so we better get started.' He helped me get up on the other guy's shoulder, my legs hanging down like goddam sticks, and then Nick went ahead, and we got started. We got about twenty yards and the guy carrying me got hit in the head. I could feel it hit him, and his head bounced against my hip, and I dropped and passed out. It knocked me out, and when I came around Nick was cussing a solid stream and trying to get me up on his back.

"'Go ahead,' I said, 'you can't make it this way.' He cussed me out for a while and said, 'Don't ever say that to me, Sergeant. Never.' So I shut up, and pretty soon I got on his back all right, up high over one shoulder, so he had one shooting arm free, and we started again. A flare went up all of a sudden, and they were shooting all around us. Nick went down on his knees, still carrying me, and waited a minute, and on the next flare he blasted in a half circle, slow to the left and back again slow, and pretty soon it was quiet out there.

"And we rested there awhile, but he wouldn't put me down. And then Nick Royal got up on his feet again, and he carried me back to the outfit and turned me in to the medics. And, as you can see, I'm here today."

Bill brought another round of drinks. I watched Schneider for a while, and then I said, "All right for the background. What about the events of this night?"

"I'll come to that," he said. "I saw Nick a few times during the rest of the war and right after, and then I didn't hear from him for twenty years, until about a month ago. He called me from Los Angeles. He said he had this organization, and it was in good shape, and he wanted a dependable man to take over details. A thousand a month to start and separation pay if I stayed six months."

"What kind of organization did he say it was?"

"Kind of combination hunting club and drill team. He was a little vague about it."

"Didn't it sound funny to you?"

"Sure, but I would have done it, for Nick."

"Did you go out there then?"

"No, I said I'd have to think it over. Then he called me a few days later and said he'd have to put the offer in reserve for a while, but stay in touch and all that.

"About four days ago he called me and said he was wiring me five hundred dollars to come to California for a special assignment. And with the trip paid for—"

"You went to California."

"Yeah, I did. I was surprised after all that time to see he hadn't changed much at all. He didn't have any gray hair, and he wasn't fat. He was the same guy I had known in that other life."

"What did he want you to do?"

"Number one, he wanted me to pick up his daughter Eloise from the college she was in—which is near Springfield—and bring her to California. He wanted to see her and he couldn't get away. Number two, he told me where he had stashed ten thousand in cash, and if anything should happen to him suddenly, I should use as much of the cash as necessary to provide for Eloise until I could turn it over to his attorney, his executor."

"Did he say what he expected to happen to him?"

"No, he wouldn't say. I asked him if I could help and he said no, nobody could help. And he gave me a paper making me guardian for Eloise, and he said, in these words: 'Don't let her go back with her mother.'"

"Probably wasn't a legal document," I said. "I doubt that a father can do it just like that."

"I don't know. I know what Nick wanted."

I threw down my slug and sent for another.

"You fascinate me," I said. "You really do."

"O.K.," he said, "we walked into that apartment and Nick Royal was there—which I didn't expect—and we got hit in the head, both of us, and knocked out. When I came around, Nick was dead and you were still out. I got up and walked away."

"Yeah," I said.

"I had to find the kid. That was the important thing."

"But you knew where the kid was, and you never showed up."

"I showed up in a few minutes. At that coffee shop—we had an arrangement about that, in case we got separated and had to get in touch—"

"What was wrong with getting in touch at the apartment?"

"The apartment was being watched."

"By who?"

"I don't know. But I know it was. Anyway, I had to walk back to the Duckblind to get my car, and I drove over to the coffee shop, and she wasn't there. I thought maybe she went to see Barnes. So I drove downtown, to the hotel, and when I got there, the cops were coming in to see Nick's brother and those people, and I couldn't hang around there. So I drove out to your place and waited."

"What did you think might happen to me?"

He shrugged.

"I figured you'd make it," he said.

I didn't know how to take it. It was a compliment, in a way, but then again—

"By the way," he said, "what did the kid do? How did you find her?"

"She found me."

I told him what she had told me. He shook his head in wonder.

"How do you like that?" he said. "Nick Royal's daughter."

"What are you going to do now?" I asked.

"I'm going to California and see that attorney—his name is Max Fisher—and try to find out what happened to Nick."

"It happened in Chicago."

"I know, but there's the kid to look after, too. I got to take one thing at a time."

I looked at him fairly hard for a while and decided he meant what he said. He was dedicated to the surviving daughter of his wartime hero. There was nothing to be done about that.

"All right," I said. "Good luck. I'll pay for the drinks."

I got out of the booth and noticed that outside it was gray with morning light.

"If you'll go along and help," he said, "I can pay you. You'd be all right with Nick."

"No, thanks," I said. "I've got a big headache, and other jobs will surely come along. So long, Schneider."

I left him in the booth, went outside and across the street, took some more aspirin and went to bed. Within seconds I was asleep.

CHAPTER 7

I was jarred out of oblivion at about eleven fifteen by a persistent knocking at my office door. It reverberated in my head like nail-studded castanets, and it made me sick to my stomach. But even after I held the pillow over my face and ears, it went on and wouldn't stop. Finally, I rolled out, stepped into my slippers, put on a bathrobe and went to the door.

There were two guys, wearing hats and conservative business suits, exuding authority—federal authority.

"Yes?" I said.

One of them brought out an ID card. It read U.S. TREASURY DE-PARTMENT. It had his name on it, but I've forgotten how to spell it.

"Come in," I said.

They came in, but they wouldn't sit down. I had to sit somewhere and settled for the corner of the desk top. One of the T-men took out some legal-looking papers and referred to them.

"We've got a routine request," he said, "to check into an organization called the League for Good Government, a transaction for firearms. The other party to the transaction is a Mr. Nat Pines, their supplier. You were involved in it."

"I was trying to collect the bill, for Nat Pines," I said.

"You're a bill collector? That's your business?"

"That's—yeah. That's what I do."

"And that was the extent of your involvement in the transaction for the firearms?"

"That's it. Incidentally, they weren't real firearms. They were toy guns."

"You saw them?"

"No. Nat Pines told me they were toy guns."

"Have you ever worked on other accounts involving this same party, the League for Good Government?"

"No. Nat said they were always good pay before."

"Did you make collection on this particular transaction?"

"Yeah. Yes, I got the money."

"Who paid it?"

"Well, the check was handed to me by a blond-haired guy named Roger. The check was made out, I think, by a woman named Gretchen Royal, and it was signed, I know, by a man named Henry Fielding."

"All these people are connected with the League for Good Government?"

"I gathered they are."

"Did you talk to anyone else in that organization?"

"One other—a man named Edgar Royal."

"Edgar Royal?"

"That's the name."

"Did you meet or have anything to do with a man named Nick Royal?"

I looked at them, one at a time, and they waited quietly.

"Nick Royal is dead," I said.

"Yes," one of them said. "We know."

"My contact with Nick Royal was very brief," I said. "About fifteen seconds."

"You never spoke to him?"

"Never."

"And you say you never actually saw any of this—merchandise for which you were trying to collect?"

"For which I did collect," I insisted.

"Excuse me," he said.

"No, I never saw the merchandise."

"Do you have any idea why this particular bill was so hard to collect, when the previous bills had all been paid promptly?"

"No," I said. "The only thing I heard anybody say was that Nick Royal had failed to take care of the matter as in the past."

"Did anybody suggest in your hearing that the reason Nick Royal had not taken care of the matter was that he had expected a shipment of real guns and had received instead a shipment of toys?"

I blinked a couple of times.

"No," I said. "Nobody suggested that."

He consulted his papers for a few seconds, folded them into his pocket and did something to the brim of his hat. "All right," he said. "Thanks for cooperating."

"No reason not to," I said.

They got to the door. One of them looked back.

"By the way, where did you see Edgar Royal?"

"In an office on LaSalle Street," I said. "The name of the organization is in the directory."

He nodded goodbye and they went out.

I went to the bedroom and stared at the bed for a while, then went to the bathroom and tried to find out from the mirror how I felt. It didn't tell me much. I washed my face with cold water and brushed my teeth and took a couple of aspirin. While I was measuring coffee into the electric pot, my telephone rang. I let it ring till it stopped; it went on ringing in my ears for three minutes. I plugged in the pot, picked up the telephone and dialed my answering service. There were several calls, some from strangers, some from people I knew but didn't want to talk to much at that time.

"And a man named Ray Barnes has been calling all morning," the girl said.

"Ray Barnes?"

"Yes. He says it's urgent."

"If it's that urgent, he could leave a message."

"He said he couldn't."

"All right, thanks. Keep taking the calls. I don't want to talk to anybody."

I sat at the desk, drinking coffee, and after a while it began to help. I wondered, but idly, whether Karl Schneider had made it to California. I couldn't see the cops, especially Sergeant Preston, letting him get out of town without talking to him. I had to admit, though, he was hard to keep track of.

I didn't want to think about him. I pushed him out of my mind, opened the door and found the morning paper. I was closing the door when a woman entered from the street, stood in the vestibule, looking lost, then latched onto me.

"Excuse me, I'm looking for a private detective named Mac—"

She was well dressed, even elegantly, in white gloves and a hat. She was in her early forties, well cared for and attractive to look at.

"Yes, ma'am," I said. "I'm the one. I'm not really dressed—"

"May I wait?"

"I guess so," I said. "Come in, please."

She came in shyly, working the white-gloved fingers of her ring hand, lifted and dropped it in one of those ambiguous feminine gestures that can signify anything from terror to acquiescent passion, and maybe all things at once.

"Would you like some coffee?" I asked.

"Thank you, that would be nice," she said. "May I sit here?"

"Certainly."

I got another cup and poured coffee for her. She took it black. I left her with it and went to the bedroom to dress. I put on slacks and a fresh shirt and left it at that. When I got back, she was sipping at the coffee. She had taken off the gloves, and they were lying on her small black purse in her lap.

"What can I do for you?" I asked.

She took her time over it, tasting the coffee and setting the cup down before she answered.

"I was wondering whether you could…find my husband for me," she said.

My spirits plunged to my slippers. One of those again.

"How long has he been gone, ma'am?" I asked.

Her handsome brow creased vertically and she counted on her naked fingers.

"Five days," she said.

"When did you expect him?"

"Five days ago," she said. "He went to New York on business, and he was to have returned last Sunday. I haven't heard from him."

"Does he drink?" I asked.

She looked suitably startled, then shook her head uncertainly.

"No, not really. Occasionally a social drink."

I felt something bad showing in my face and turned away to look out the window.

"You were highly recommended," she said. "By Mr. Harkness, George Harkness, a lawyer we know."

I knew George Harkness a little, not much.

"Thank you," I said. "But, ma'am—by the way, what is your name?"

"Peterson," she said. "Naomi Peterson. My husband's name is Ralph."

"Did Mr. Harkness take any steps himself?"

"Yes, he said he did all the…usual things. He checked the airlines, reservations and that sort of thing, and got in touch with all my husband's business associates and acquaintances—"

"Both here and in New York?"

"Yes, I believe so."

"And nothing turned up?"

"No."

There was a major pause. It hurt quite a lot, but it probably hurt her more than it did me.

"Mr. Harkness said you could find him if anyone could. He gave me the impression you could do almost anything you set your mind to."

"He flatters me," I said.

I swung slowly in my chair and tried to face her.

"I might possibly be able to find him," I said. "Most people aren't really hard to find, if you're serious—"

Karl Schneider? I thought.

"But," I said, "suppose I do?"

Her eyes widened and she lifted that hand.

"I guess I don't know what you mean."

"Look," I said, "I don't want to hurt you, but I don't want you to spend a lot of money—without telling you that finding him may be only part of the job."

She shook her head in that vague way.

"Assuming your husband hasn't come to harm, isn't sick or something—which you would have learned by now if it were true—why wouldn't he have got in touch with you, to let you know he'd be delayed?"

"Well…I really can't say…why he wouldn't—"

"One reason could be that he doesn't want to."

Her only reaction was to shift her eyes slightly and look into some secret space beyond me.

"You mean," she said, "he may be leaving me."

"Maybe not permanently."

I began to hate myself.

"If he is leaving me," she said, with elegant firmness, "I think I would like to know."

Someone knocked at the door, sharp and impatient. I started to say something and the knock came again, louder and more impatient.

"Excuse me," I said.

I went to the door and opened it. There was a man outside, well dressed, about forty, maybe younger, wearing glasses and a neat beard.

"I'm busy right now," I said. "You'll have to wait or come back later."

He frowned above the bridge of the glasses.

"How long—"

"I don't know," I said.

"I'll wait," he said, backing away.

I started back into the office, then went out to the vestibule, pulling the door shut behind me.

"Would your name by any chance be Peterson?" I asked. "Ralph Peterson?"

"No," he said abruptly. "Barnes. Ray Barnes."

"Oh," I said.

I went back to the office, and Naomi Peterson was pulling on her gloves.

"Will you try to find him?" she asked.

"One more thing I have to ask you," I said. "If I should try, and if I find him, will you expect me to deliver him to you? Persuade him to come home—if he doesn't want to?"

She looked me straight in the eye, and hers didn't flinch.

"No," she said. "I wouldn't expect that."

"All right," I said, "I'll do what I can. Can I get the basic information from Mr. Harkness?"

"Yes, I think that would be best."

"All right. I'll call him."

"Will it be very expensive? Will you have to go to New York?"

"Probably not," I said. "Certainly not now. I'll let you know how the expenses are going."

"Thank you," she said. "Thanks for being honest with me."

I shrugged.

"Good luck, Mrs. Peterson," I said.

"The same to you," she said.

She left the office as coolly as she had come in. I kind of hated to see her go. She was good for my morale.

Mr. Ray Barnes, I calculated, had come near running her down in his hurry to get in. He was readjusting the nosepiece of his glasses en route, and he was in an extremely uptight condition.

"Sit down, Mr. Barnes," I said. "Have a cup of coffee."

"No, thanks," he said. "I want to talk to you about Eloise Royal."

"Okay," I said, "talk."

He wouldn't sit down, so I didn't either, though not by way of politeness. I didn't like the way he fidgeted.

"I thought, perhaps," he said, "as you found a way to get rid of her, you could find a way to get her back."

I poured myself some more coffee.

"I didn't know I had found a way to get rid of her," I said, "and I certainly don't want her back."

"That's not what I mean," he said, "and you know it."

I drank some of the coffee.

"I wish you'd sit down," I said.

He didn't like it, but he sat down, on the forward edge of a straight chair with his hands on his knees.

"Now, about Eloise—" I said.

"Eloise told you she didn't want to rejoin her mother," he said.

"She said something like that, yes."

"And she told you she wanted to get in touch with me, Ray Barnes."

"I believe so. She also told me you were her boyfriend. Now that I meet you, I'm thinking about that."

"What about that?"

"She's seventeen years old."

"Don't be moralistic with me—"

"Not moralistic. I know these matches sometimes work out—young girl, older man. But not very often, and usually back in the hills."

"Eloise is an unusually mature girl—"

"No," I said, "she's an unusually immature girl. But aside from that, when the juvenile officers came for her, the issue was cut-and-dried. No argument. Back to her mother she went."

His effort at self-control was so violent that he dislodged his glasses, and took time to replace them.

"One thing you may not know," he said. "Her mother doesn't care about her, not in the least. She wants her only for her own purposes."

"I wouldn't know about that," I said. "But it doesn't change much, does it?"

"It makes a large difference to me!"

"There's something else you know—or knew—that nobody else knew. That Nick Royal was in Chicago. You knew it before Karl Schneider, before Gretchen, even before Eloise. How did you know?"

"That's beside the point—"

"It's not beside the point as far as the cops are concerned."

"I have nothing to do with that."

"Then you can explain it."

That big, phony control act again, but he kept the glasses on his nose.

"I'm under the impression that it's I who is owed explanations—"

"Oh, shove it," I said. "You've got a hot thing for a chick young enough to be your daughter, and you're blowing your cool at both ends. I couldn't explain the time of day to you."

He came up off the chair, and I swear he was shaking. He took off his glasses and stuffed them in his breast pocket, and I had a momentary impression he was about to challenge me to a duel.

"Eloise was right," he said through his teeth. "She told me you were a fink—a sellout fink."

"Man, like you're right," I said.

But he was all the way turned off. He confronted me with squirming lips for about five and a half seconds, then turned and stalked—I mean *stalked*—to the door and went out. He slammed it, but not very hard.

Wrong guy, Eloise, I thought.

I don't want to think about Eloise, I told myself. There's chores to be done.

I was hungry now, and I didn't feel like eating a piece of cheese on a slab of stale bread. I felt like having a hot dish of soup at Tony's.

I found George Harkness' number in the phone book and dialed it. A lady came on, and after a while I was connected with the boss. I told him who was calling, and he was right there.

"Oh, yes," he said. "Mrs. Peterson saw you?"

"Uh-huh," I said. "Have you got a file on the basic stuff?"

"Sure. You want me to send it to you?"

"No, I'll pick it up, if you'll leave it with your girl."

"Sure," he said. "What time?"

"Any time."

"All right. Thanks for seeing her."

"She's a nice lady. I like them like her."

"Who doesn't?" he said.

"I guess Ralph Peterson doesn't."

"Don't jump to conclusions."

"O.K." I said. "Thanks for the referral."

"Any time," he said.

I hung up and dialed again, and a man answered, a man with quite a lot of special know-how. His name was Artie Candle, and you can't beat a name like that.

"Artie," I said, "I need some background on a guy named Ralph Peterson."

"Ralph Peterson who?"

"That's all I got. He's married. He's in business. He lives here and takes business trips. His wife's name is Naomi."

"Yeah," Artie said. "See you around."

"Thank you, sir."

He replied to that, but it's not important to the story.

I went to the back room, shaved myself with the electric razor and put on some clean socks and some relatively clean shoes, a necktie and jacket and a hat I hadn't worn for several months. It seemed to fit all right, which was comforting. I hesitated at the desk, started to lift the phone to call the answering service, changed my mind and walk out to the vestibule. There were some throwaways on the floor, and I picked them up and dumped them in the trash basket near the front door. I had opened the door and started down the steps when Edgar Royal came charging up at me, off balance, and nearly broke his nose against the glass in the west panel. He would have broken his nose if I hadn't caught him.

CHAPTER 8

The birthmark on his face and neck was livid. He was panting, and there were beads of sweat on his forehead. Behind his glasses, his eyes were coated with sheen. He stuck his finger at me, almost hitting me in the mouth. "You—" he said. "You set the cops on me!"

"I did?" I said.

"The feds—the Treasury men."

"Oh, them."

I wondered what was really bugging him, to get him in such a state. It couldn't be a visit from the T-men—unless he really had something going on, which I doubted.

"They came on a routine check-out," I said. "I didn't know they had anything on you."

"They haven't—not a thing, not anything at all. And you knew it—"

"Then you're all right," I said. "What's the sweat?"

He took time to pull up some strings. It wasn't easy for him, but he got his voice down, and his eyes were less glazed when he said, "I think I've figured it out. You and Nick—you and my brother Nick were working together."

I stared at him.

"I don't think you've got it figured out at all," I said. "I never even heard of your brother Nick till you mentioned him yesterday afternoon."

"You and that other private eye—Schneider."

"You mean all three of us were working together?"

"It has to be," he said, talking to himself now.

He might not be far off to think Schneider and Nick had been working together, but I decided not to encourage him.

"Listen," I said, "would you like to come in and have a belt? It's hot out here in the noonday sun."

He backed away and nearly fell down the steps.

"That's all right," he said. "You take care of yourself, and I'll be all right. I've still got friends."

"I'm glad to hear it," I said.

I watched him down the steps and along the street toward Michigan, a drunken progress, a guy on the bad run.

I went on down to the street and crossed slowly over to Tony's. I talked one of the early waitresses into fixing me some eggs and toast, a meal that is not pushed at Tony's at any time, let alone in the afternoon. But I was a good customer.

I ordered a glass of beer to wait with, and when it came, I got up and went to the phone booth in the back. I dialed the Palmer House and asked for Ed Croft. This time, though there was a delay, there was no argument. I hoped good old Ed had got himself some sleep.

"Yeh… Hey, I just tried to call you," he said, coming on a little breathless.

"You got me now," I said. "Go ahead."

"That Ray Barnes, remember?"

"I remember."

"He came in about ten minutes ago, like he was flying, and went up to his room, and about five minutes ago, he had a couple of visitors."

"Like who?"

"Bad guys. One of them I think I know from far back—guy named Ludowicz, they call him Ludwig. The other one was some gorilla I never saw before, guy about eight feet tall."

"Are they still there, with Barnes?"

"Haven't come down yet. I spotted them because they were hanging around the lobby, waiting, and when Barnes came in, they went right up without phoning or anything, so naturally I checked it out and it was Barnes's room they went to."

"Well—" I said.

I had my hand in my pocket, and I pulled it out and looked at a crumpled $50 bill, the one I'd forgotten to give back to Schneider.

"You want me to do anything about them?" Ed was saying.

"It's not my case," I said. "I don't know."

I kept looking at the fifty.

I've earned it in backlash alone, I thought.

"Is there any way you can delay them?" I asked him. "When they come down, if you can hold them a few minutes, I'll try to make it down there. I'm at Tony's."

"I'll try," he said. "Make it quick."

"What about the Royal party—and Fielding?" I asked.

"All gone. Checked out."

"How come the police let 'em go?"

"I don't know. It's a little mysterious. One cop told me they didn't have enough on anybody to hold them up."

"All right. I'll be along."

Back at my table the waitress was serving the eggs and toast.

"Sorry, baby," I said, snatching a gulp of beer, "no time to eat."

"You lousy—" she hissed.

"I'll pay for 'em. You eat 'em. Eggs are good for you."

"Eggs I got," she growled. "You want to come up and fertilize them sometime?"

I let that pass. Any answer would have been the wrong one. I did give her a quick kiss on the ear and left the joint to get to my car.

* * * *

There was a jam just north of the Michigan Avenue bridge, and I lost about six minutes in it, so I didn't make the Palmer House till almost half an hour after Ed had talked to me. I could tell by his face when I got to him that the birds had flown.

"I held them up for a few minutes," he said, "but they were jumpy, and it was the best I could do. Jesus, that big guy!"

"Any idea what they wanted with Barnes?"

"No. They didn't stay long."

"Barnes is still in?"

"I guess so."

"This Mr. Ludwig—would I know about him?"

"Maybe. He's been around for years, kind of a freelance, lone-wolf goon squad. He gets a job, he hires a crew for it. I never saw the big guy before."

"You know where Mr. Ludwig hangs out?"

"I think I can get it for you."

"Give it a try. I'll go up and see Barnes."

He gave me Barnes' room number.

"What happened to Karl Schneider?" Ed asked.

"The last I heard, he was heading for California."

Ed's eyebrows did a shuffle.

"They let him go, too?"

"Yeah. I can't help thinking they've got a tail on them or something. Got to have. Donovan's in on it now."

"Yeah?" I said.

"O.K., I'll go look up about Ludwig."

I got in an elevator, went up to the sixth floor and found Barnes' room. When I knocked, he snarled from deep inside.

"What is it now?"

I cupped my mouth with one hand and tried to remember the Polish accent from my boyhood days.

"It's me—Mr. Loodvix—forgot something."

His voice was closer, but still inside the room.

"I gave you the money. We're square. I'm busy now."

I had half turned to leave when the door opened. I turned back to look at him. His mouth was working, and those glasses were bouncing around on his nose.

"You—" he growled.

"What did you pay Mr. Ludwig for?" I asked.

He glared at me while I counted silently to four; then he slammed the door shut. I want back to the elevator, and down in the lobby I looked up Ed Croft.

"I got Ludwig's residence address," he said. "South Side."

"Good for you."

He handed me an empty match folder with a blank inside space, where he had written an address. I looked at it and put it in my pocket.

"Watch out for the big one," he said.

"Uh-huh," I said.

"And fill me in, huh?"

"You know me," I said.

* * * *

It was in the old Hull House neighborhood. There had been some changes through the years, but a few classic tenements remained, dry and dusty in the yellow daylight. The one I was looking for stood five stories high and had iron balustrades on the front steps. An old man was sitting on the steps, smoking a pipe, reading a racing form.

In the frayed vestibule were mailboxes on which the locks no longer functioned. Half of them were stuffed with junk mail that hadn't been picked up for days. Most of them bore no names, but over box number 208 was the name "Ludwig, P."

A wide staircase rose from just inside the double glass-paneled door. There was a more than usually spacious landing on the second floor; a balustrade ran the width of the building, and the stairs continued upward on the opposite side of the landing. The second floor hall narrowed back from the landing area.

I used to live in one of these, I thought. I really did.

I climbed to the landing. A fat woman in a heavy shapeless sweater came down from above, bumping a two-wheeled shopping cart behind her. I made way for her and went along the hall looking for 208. It was the last room on the left at the rear. A white card pasted to the door panel read MR. LUDWIG. There were no sounds I could hear, but I could smell cooking food. The location of food odors in a tenement, however, is often uncertain. I knocked, rather firmly, and after a while I knocked again.

I was leaning against the wall near the door, waiting, when a judas window opened in the door across the hall, and somebody looked out at me.

Remarkably low crime rate in tenement districts, I thought. Someone is always watching.

I stared back, and finally the little window closed. I tried Mr. Ludwig's doorknob; it was locked, and I knocked again. The door opened across the hall, and two young men came out. The hall was only a scant four feet wide here, and for fifteen feet toward the front, where it broadened into the landing. I flattened against the wall next to Mr. Ludwig's door to let them pass. They wore cheap, sharp suits and their hair far down the backs of their necks. One of them was dark-skinned, with a white scar across his left cheek. The other was almost white-haired, heavyset, on the pudgy side. They walked to where the hall opened up, then stopped, faced about and looked at me.

"Who you want?" the dark one asked.

I turned to the door and knocked again.

"He don't answer," the dark one said.

The other one giggled.

"He ain't going to answer," he said. "He ain't home."

I looked at the back of my hand.

"Just go ahead and wait," the dark one said. "He'll come back."

The pudgy one emitted another giggle.

"Thank you very much," I said.

"That's all right," the pudgy one said.

They went away, and I could hear their heels hitting hard on the old wood flooring.

Oh, boy, I thought.

I gave them time to get downstairs and out of the building, then turned my back on Mr. Ludwig's door and started away. I got as far as the end of the narrow part of the hall, and a door opened behind me.

"Something you wanted?" a man's voice said.

I looked around and a roly-poly guy with a haircut like a monk's and a dark brown robe to match was looking at me from Mr. Ludwig's doorway. The light gleamed on the top of his bald skull. He had a round nose, laced with blue veins, and small eyes that you couldn't tell about from a distance.

"Mr. Ludwig?" I said.

"Yes. I was asleep. I hope you didn't wait too long."

"Not quite," I said.

I went back toward the open door. Mr. Ludwig didn't make any way for me, and his bulk more or less filled the opening.

"I'm looking for Ray Barnes," I said.

"I'm afraid I can't help you," he said.

"You're acquainted with Ray Barnes?"

"Are you asking me or telling me?"

"I'm asking," I said.

"I guess I don't have that pleasure," he said.

Inside the room, a telephone began to ring.

"You'll have to excuse me," he said, backing off.

I couldn't see much past him except some faded wallpaper with pink flowers on it. The telephone rang again. Mr. Ludwig began to close the door, and I put my knee against it.

"I'll wait," I said. "Go ahead and answer the phone."

Mr. Ludwig's little eyes came into a hard focus.

"That won't help," he said. "Please let me close the door."

I moved farther into the opening that remained and said, "I'm not here to make trouble. Just some information."

Mr. Ludwig's eyes, I discovered, were a burned charcoal color, with flecks of pink in them. They didn't rest on me long. He shrugged his round shoulders under the robe and gave up, backing into the room. I went along. The telephone was still ringing. At a glance, the room was not badly furnished, but a glance was all I had time for. From a wing chair near the back wall, out of sight from the hall, a man was getting on his feet, dropping the sports section of the *Tribune* as he rose.

He rose for what seemed forever, till he got to be about seven feet tall. He had lots of shoulders, long thick arms and practically no waist at all. He was wearing a T-shirt and a pair of purple slacks, and his hands were the size of medium large skillets. He was balder than Mr. Ludwig. He was as bald as a streetlamp, the bulb in which he could have changed without standing on tiptoe. The telephone rang in my head like an air raid alert.

Answer it! I thought.

The big guy stood there, looking down at me. It was a little like being in the woods and having an oak tree look at you. Mr. Ludwig had picked up a telephone and, standing in his fat robe, was speaking into it. The big one took a step toward me, and I hopped backward, holding up both hands.

"I quit," I said.

Mr. Ludwig was saying, "There's a gentleman here right now, in fact. He didn't introduce himself."

I was having some trouble with my breath. I wished the conversation would end. Then I wished it wouldn't, not yet.

"I see," Ludwig said, "what do you want me to do?…For how long?"

He's talking to Barnes, I decided.

"Just a minute," Mr. Ludwig said.

He laid the instrument down, walked back to within about six feet of me and peered at me. His charcoal eyes didn't change. Pretty soon he went back to the phone.

The aroma of the cooking food was sharp in my nose. It smelled like chicken.

"I think that is the one," Ludwig said.

The giant was growing restless, moving his hands, also, somewhat, his eyes, as if tired of standing in one place. The only thing like a weapon that I could see was a wooden kitchen chair at a dinette table about three paces to my right and a little behind me. It would be too fragile to depend on, unless I could stick it in his eyes. The apartment door was still open and there was the possibility, I told myself, of luring him out to the landing, where there would be more space. But—

"Very good," Mr. Ludwig was saying to the phone. "I understand."

He hung up, and the big bastard eyed me like a gourmet eyeing a feast. He was big enough, I thought. With a little aid from Ludwig, he could have knocked Schneider and me out and handled the knifing of Nick Royal, too.

Why? I wondered.

He shuffled his feet, and I backed off, a half step nearer that wooden chair.

"We're not to harm him, Lawrence," Mr. Ludwig said mildly.

Lawrence just stared at me. Remembering the distance to the door, I figured I had a two-pace jump on him. It didn't seem like much.

"He's to stay here for a short time," Ludwig said. "Then he's free to go."

Ludwig walked away toward the kitchen. The big guy's eyes followed him. I stepped back and a little right, grabbed the top rail of the kitchen chair and broke for the door. Lawrence jumped for me. I threw the chair at his head and got into the hall. I could hear his feet banging behind me as I headed for the balustrade at the edge of the landing. When I looked around he was coming straight at me, and I feinted toward the down staircase, then pivoted back to my left. It threw him off enough to gain me half a second on him. By the time he made the switch, I was behind him.

I wasn't quite close enough to the stairs, so I tried for the balustrade. I kicked the back of his right knee and pushed with both hands in the small of his back. He fell into the rail, which was built better than it should have been and didn't give way. He went pretty far over it, but not quite far enough. He came back, twisting and reaching for me, and I ducked very low and hit him three times in the soft place under his ribs and managed to get clear of his flailing arms. He was very angry now. At the top of the stairs he came at me like a wild windmill. He caught me on the side of the head and knocked me into the wall. I bounced back to my left, and when he turned to get at me, I banged into him from the side and shouldered him off balance. Then I hit the small of his back once more, and he tumbled down the stairs. It made a sound like nearby thunder.

I looked around, and Mr. Ludwig was standing at the end of the narrow back hall, holding a carving knife in one hand and a steaming chicken on a fork in the other.

"Come here," I said.

My ear was still ringing on the side where Lawrence had clouted me, and I couldn't hear myself talk, so I said it again, louder, and gestured. He came toward me slowly in his fat robe, holding that damn chicken on the end of the fork. I pointed down the steps at where Lawrence was slowly hauling himself into a semi-upright position.

"What kind of job did you do for Ray Barnes?" I asked him.

Ludwig peered down the steps and didn't answer.

"Come on," I said. "I'll throw you down there too."

I moved toward him, and he did a kind of hop and skip away from me, causing the chicken to swing jerkily on the fork.

"It was merely a stakeout," he said. "For purposes of observation."

"What were you supposed to observe?"

He glanced down the stairs. Lawrence had started up, hanging onto the rail with one hand, shaking his big bald head.

"Come on up," I said, beckoning with both hands.

He stopped, looking up at me.

"What was the object of your attention?" I asked Ludwig.

I took another step toward him, and he threatened me with the carving knife. I reached out and batted it out of his hand. The chicken wobbled frantically on the fork, and Ludwig extended his empty hand to steady it.

"It was an apartment hotel on the South Side," he said.

"The Venetian Arms?"

"That was the name, yes."

I wished my ear would stop ringing. I looked at the stairs, and Lawrence was coming up again, but very slowly.

"What did you see at the Venetian Arms?" I asked.

"Well, there were certain people, coming and going—"

"Like Karl Schneider?" I said. "Eloise Royal?"

"I believe those were the names, yes."

"And you saw Nick Royal go in there, too?"

"A large man, with curly hair—yes."

"Was Ray Barnes with you at the time?"

He had begun to shake under the robe. Everything jiggled, including the chicken.

"From time to time, as I remember."

"Was he there at the time Karl Schneider and I entered the building?"

"Well, I'm not too clear in my head—"

"Get clear. Which one of you stuck the knife in Nick Royal?"

He glanced at the floor where the carving knife was lying.

"Oh, no, nothing like that," he said.

"Was it Barnes?"

"Not that I saw, no. We weren't there to do any such thing—"

Lawrence was getting close to the landing, and I had to attend to him. I went over there, and he stopped again. I picked up the carving knife and gave him another come-on. He came on, one step at a time. Behind me there were sudden footsteps. Ludwig had made a break for the back hall. I started after him, then changed my mind. The big guy hit the landing, and I swung back, holding the long knife well out.

"Clear through you," I said.

But he was gazing past me toward the hall. I glanced that way and saw Ludwig turn and lunge for the door. He hit his shoulder against the jamb, and the chicken fell off the fork onto the floor. He stared down at it for a moment, then leaned over, reaching with the fork, and picked it up again. I watched Lawrence, his eyes on the hall, walk past me slowly, heading for home.

The hell with it, I thought. It's not my case.

I went down the steps and out of the building and drove a couple of blocks. Then I stopped and went into a phone booth. I dialed the Palmer House and finally got hold of Ed Croft.

"Is Barnes still there?" I asked him.

"No, he checked out. Air transport."

"California."

"I guess so."

"All right, thanks."

"What happened with Ludwig?" he asked.

"The hell with it," I said.

I hung up, left the booth and then returned to it. I dialed police head-quarters—which from where I stood was a few scant blocks away—and got the homicide squad room. A guy answered, and I asked for Lieutenant Donovan.

"Went out for lunch," he said.

"Zinty's?"

"I guess so. Where else?"

I hung up and got back into the car.

CHAPTER 9

Zinty's, in the shadow of the South State Street establishment for law enforcement, looked even dingier than I remembered it. I went in by the front door, and there were half a dozen guys in uniform at the coffee shop counter. Farther back, at the beer bar, sat a couple of old detectives I knew by sight. Zinty was tending bar.

"Donovan?" I said.

He stabbed his thumb toward the back room. I went through a curtained opening. Donovan was sitting alone at one of three tables covered with red and white oilcloth. Beer cartons were stacked against two of the walls. There was a candle on Donovan's table, but it wasn't lighted. He sat with his chin in one hand, wearing his glasses, reading the paper.

I sat down across from him, and he went on reading the paper.

"About the murder of Nick Royal—" I said.

He didn't even lift his eyes.

"That's Joe Preston's case," he said.

"Yeah, and I'm the only suspect available."

He grunted something.

"All the others," I said, "have blown town."

He got to the end of whatever he was reading, took off his glasses and gazed out the dirty window.

"Well," he said, "the governor of California called the governor of Illinois and said, 'Let my people go.' So that's how all that happened."

He eyed his paper furtively, but I felt like hanging on. This was a major question in my mind.

"You got some kind of a tail on them?" I said.

He shrugged.

"Like this," he said. "There wasn't anything on them. Edgar Royal was in his office most all night, and he had company, which we checked out. Mr. Fielding and Mrs. Royal were at the hotel, and we got that confirmed, too. Schneider—we never even saw him. All we know about him is what you said. On top of all this these people are very big in California, and there was a lot of pressure on us. We had to let 'em go."

"Those two musclemen, too?" I said. "The two in the white shirts?"

He had put his glasses back on and turned a page of the paper. Now he took them off and looked at me again—for quite a while.

"What two musclemen?" he said.

"Fielding had a bodyguard," I said. "They hung around the hotel. Anyway, part of the time. One was named Roger, and the other one had a name like Brick—or Schtick or something. Boys with hard hands."

He groped in his pocket and came up with a toothpick. It moved from side to side of his mouth.

"Why didn't you mention them before?" he asked.

"Nobody asked me. Nobody asked me anything."

He snapped the toothpick into two pieces and dropped them on the floor.

"You know a man called Mr. Ludwig?" I asked.

"Yeah—Ludowicz, the 'Polish terror.'"

"He and an assistant about the size of the Wrigley Building were staked out on the building where Royal was killed. Last night. Most of the night."

"You don't say," he said.

"The big one is big enough to have done the whole trick by himself alone. I don't know if he's smart enough, but he's big enough and strong enough."

"Ludowicz?" Donovan said, gazing dreamily through the window. "Ludowicz wouldn't have balls enough to hire out for murder."

"Maybe he didn't know what he was getting into."

"Who hired him?" Donovan asked.

"Man named Ray Barnes, a professor at the state college near Springfield. He checked out of the Palmer House awhile ago."

"To go where?"

"California."

Donovan nodded glumly.

"All right," he said. "I'll tell Preston. I guess we could get Barnes picked up in California if we have to. He don't belong to that Royal outfit, does he?"

"No."

"Then I guess we could get him picked up."

"That's all I know now," I said. "Goodbye."

"So long," Donovan said, and picked up his paper.

I got as far as the curtain, and he called me back.

"If Barnes has got no connection with the Royals," he said, "why would he kill Nick Royal?"

"He's sort of connected. He's in love with Nick Royal's daughter."

Donovan blinked.

"That little kid?"

"Little bundle of wild, wild woman," I said.

"How old is Barnes?" he said.

"About forty."

"Maybe we could pick him up for child-molesting."

"I don't know," I said. "I never saw him molest her."

"O.K."

"See you around," I said.

I started the car once more and drove to George Harness' office in the Loop. He wasn't in, but his girl had a bundle of papers for me. I thanked her, stuffed them up under my arm and went out and found a place to get something to eat in. The file on Ralph Peterson was a miscellaneous scattering of notes, mostly in longhand. Harkness had made some effort to organize them, but they were still fairly helter-skelter. There was a list of the names of his immediate business associates, with telephone numbers and street addresses. There were notes on his hotel reservations and records of calls to the hotel in New York, which he had checked out of five days before. He had relatives in New York; all of them had been listed, and Harkness recorded calls to most of them; the others were marked DNA. His round-trip airline reservation had been marked: "Arrived, 11 a.m. Tucs.—no departure, res. *not* canceled." Harkness had done a thorough job. The only thing he had overlooked, a possibility that would occur automatically to any self-respecting skip tracer, was automobile rental agencies. He had remembered, however, to include a detailed description of Peterson and a photograph. A good-looking guy, nearing fifty, with plenty of hair and good teeth.

Over coffee, I wrote out a telegram, giving Peterson's description, the time of his scheduled departure from New York and his business connection—he was a manufacturer's representative for a line of high-quality sound equipment—and at the end of the information, I wrote: "Check out car rentals two days around given departure date." I addressed it to a skip tracer named Maury Callahan in New York City and phoned it in from the restaurant telephone before I left.

At home I called the answering service. There had been a call from Donovan, but it was earlier than the time I had seen him, so I let that go. Also, Mrs. Ralph Peterson had called. I let that go, too, because it was a lot too soon for her to expect any results, and I had dealt with anxious wives in the past and didn't feel up to dealing with one at the moment. As a matter of fact, all I felt up to was a nap, and I lay down on the office couch at four thirty-eight and didn't wake up until half past seven. This time when I checked the answering service, there was more action. For one thing, Artie Candle had called. I called him back, and it went like this:

"Mac, hey—Peterson, Ralph, right?"

"Right," I said.

"Born Indianapolis forty-nine years ago, married Naomi Green 1947, no children, manufactured amplifiers and other components, sold out 1956 to New York outfit which he now represents—"

"I got all that, Artie, thanks. What else?"

"O.K. Orderly life, no ladies' man, steady, attends annual reunion USMC Officers' WW-two; lived on Delaware Near North Side till 1952, now in Glencoe—"

"Hold it, Artie—about those reunions?"

"Uh—yeah, Marine Corps officers—"

"World War Two?"

"Yeah, something?"

"I don't know. Go ahead."

"Not much more. Peterson's not a rich man but well off, pays his bills. Goes to big electronics show Merchandise Mart twice a year and makes New York once a year for sales meetings and stuff like that. I got nothing on him in New York."

"All right, good job, Artie, thanks. How much? I'll send you a check."

"Thirty bucks, Mac, all right?"

"All right."

He hung up, and I went in and washed and changed my shirt, made myself a drink in the kitchen and walked around drinking it. At eight fifteen the answering service called with a telegram from Maury Callahan in New York. It read: "Peterson rented Hertz car Manhattan, Saturday, turned it in at Philadelphia late Saturday; booked nonscheduled flight Burbank, California, Sunday a.m. More question mark. P.S., Coast-to-Coast Airlines."

Maury always left something out until the last minute, and he would tack it on the end rather than rewrite the message. It gave his reports an exhilarating spontaneity.

I sent him a wire reading: "No more now, Maury, thanks. Bill me."

I thought about it for a few minutes and dialed Mrs. Peterson's number. She came on right away. And she had something to say.

"I'm glad you called. After I left you this morning, I was reading the paper...about this murder last night, a man named Nick Royal?"

"Yes," I said.

"Well, Ralph used to talk about a Marine he knew during the war—World War Two, that is—I'm quite sure it's the same man. I never met him myself."

"Has your husband spoken about him recently, in the last few weeks?" I asked.

"No, not that I remember. But I do remember the name, and that Ralph spoke about him with quite a lot of enthusiasm."

"All right."

She evidently wasn't making the easy hysterical connection between her husband and his old buddy and the fact that one of them was now dead and the other missing. That was a relief. She was quite a woman.

"That may not mean anything," she said wistfully.

"It may mean quite a lot," I said. "I have learned that your husband went from New York to California. I haven't had a report from California yet. But Nick Royal was from California, and it might just be that they had some arrangement to see each other."

"But why wouldn't he tell me?"

"I don't know. Unless it was something he thought you would...worry about, and if he planned to be gone for a couple of days—"

"Yes, but—"

"Let me get something from California, and I'll call you back right away."

"All right, thank you," she said and hung up.

I sat there with my hand on the phone and wished somebody would bring me another drink. There was a steady humming in my ears. It resembled the hum of a jet plane in flight.

I called a detective agency in Hollywood and hung on till they got me in touch with the guy I wanted, a guy named Jackson Rivers. I gave him what I had and asked for an urgent report. I hung up, got myself another drink, returned to the desk and sat there until the phone rang. It was Rivers.

"Peterson arrived Burbank airport noon Sunday," he said. "He didn't hire a car. He had one suitcase with him. No trace. You want me to get on it?"

"Not right this minute," I said. "I'll call you or something."

"O.K., Mac," he said.

I sat there until the drink was gone and the summer night had closed down outside. Then I used the phone again and after some time got connected with Lieutenant Joe Preston.

"Is the heat still on me?" I asked him.

"Why do you ask?" he said.

"I've got an assignment that might send me out of town."

"How far out?"

"California," I said.

He didn't say anything.

"How did you make out with that stuff I gave Donovan?" I asked.

"Ludowicz?" he said. "Not much so far."

"Maybe it's nothing," I said, stalling, waiting for him to make the move.

"About those two muscleboys you mentioned," he said. "How did they get out of sight so soon?"

"I don't know. There was quite an interval there while I was unconscious and you were checking out this and that."

There was quite a long pause.

"You entertaining some slight suspicion," I said, "that I got into something with this Nick Royal and stabbed him to death?"

Another pause.

"Let me put it this way," he said. "I would never figure you to do a thing like that. On the other hand, we've got nobody else but you."

"I didn't do it," I said.

"I'm glad if it's true," he said.

"Can I go to California? I'm bonded."

"How can I keep you from going to California?"

"Oh," I said, "you might find a way, if you wanted to."

"Yeah," he said.

Now it was the lieutenant who was stalling. I wondered why, but I wasn't sure I really wanted to know.

"Well," he said, "if it becomes necessary for you to go to California, check in with me."

"All right, Lieutenant," I said.

I called Mrs. Peterson.

"I have traced your husband to Burbank, California," I said. "I can try to hire a detective out there—I know at least one good one. Or I can go myself. It will cost around two fifty for the round trip, and expenses seventy-five dollars a day. The California detective would charge the same daily rate, but there wouldn't be any transportation expense."

"I'd prefer that you do it yourself," she said. "I don't care about the expense."

"All right, then, I'll report," I said.

"Thank you. I do hope you find him."

"Yes, ma'am," I said. "So do I."

I called both airports and found there were no flights to Burbank until some time the next day. I could get to Los Angeles around three in the morning, if I could make the flight. I confirmed the reservation for Los Angeles and went to the bedroom to pack a bag. I got the chore started all right but I couldn't work up any enthusiasm for it. I still had three hours until flight time and hanging around airports with time to spare is not my favorite form of recreation. Tony's was a better place to hang around. So I left the suitcase open, walked across the street and filled myself in on the neighborhood gossip while sipping a couple of slugs of whisky on the rocks. The gossip was dull, but the place was warm and friendly and the tone was peaceful. I whiled away something more than an hour in this fashion and eventually, reluctantly, made my way home. I was putting my razor and toilet kit into the suitcase when the office door began to rattle and when I opened it, Lieutenants Preston and Donovan were standing in the hall.

Two lieutenants at one time form an impressive visitation. I stepped back, fighting an impulse to bow, and let them in.

Preston felt it necessary to explain.

"One of the best things the headquarters communication system does," he said, "is to keep in touch with the airports."

"All right," I said. "Make yourselves comfortable."

CHAPTER 10

They decided not to have a drink with me. Donovan was the senior officer, so he got to do the talking. The first thing he said was, "Planning to skip town?"

"No," I said. "I talked to Lieutenant Preston about it. I got an assignment—"

"But you were to check in with Lieutenant Preston. You went ahead and made a reservation, at Midway, for tonight."

"There wasn't going to be any point in checking with Lieutenant Preston if I couldn't get out of town anyway—"

I couldn't figure out why they were giving me a bad time, except that they were both in a bad mood. One reason for the bad mood could be that their case had gone wrong, that they had been let down by the real big shots, such as the governor and probably the D.A., and as a result they were badly frustrated and felt like losers. There was also a possibility that they actually thought I was mixed up in some way with Schneider or Royal and was holding out on them. There wasn't anything I could do for them on either count. I could only ride out the storm.

"How come you didn't say anything to me about these two goons or whatever they were, the two that hung around Fielding and Mrs. Royal?" Preston said. "I mean when I was on the scene there and you were telling me what happened."

"I forgot about them," I said. "It didn't come up, I mean, I hadn't put that much together at that time."

"What have you put together now?" Donovan said.

"Nothing. All I know is that I saw these two at the hotel and they acted like bodyguards. I figure it took two at least to bang Schneider up like that. But I don't know it was them."

"Ed Croft at the Palmer House told us," Donovan said, "that you called him on the phone while we were in the middle of the investigation. What was that about?"

"It was about this guy Barnes, and the girl, Eloise, who had picked me up there—"

"You didn't call in about the girl."

"I..."

I cut myself off. Everything I said made it worse. They were after me for something, and I would have to find out what it was before I would know what to say.

"I give up," I said. "What do you want from me?"

They studied me from two angles. It was a rough study that didn't exactly warm the cockles of my heart.

"All of them took off for California. Barnes took off for California. Schneider flew to California early this morning. Now you."

I stared at them.

"You were in that apartment with Royal," Preston said, "with the murder knife practically in your hand. You had Royal's blood all over you. When the juvenile people caught up with the Royal girl, they caught up with you at the same time."

Donovan was looking at me head on, his eyes far back and flat, his big jaw set crookedly.

"You're in it, Mac."

I was beginning to get scared. I couldn't make myself believe that Donovan would do this to me. The case couldn't hold up through a trial, could it? But they could use me to pry the thing open. It's been done before when there was a reluctant prosecutor. You throw him something he doesn't want, and he comes through with the assistance; he starts breaking down doors for you. Meanwhile, the one that gets thrown in has a rough time of it. The cops have to make it look real, and sometimes—I didn't want to think along those lines.

"O.K.," I said, "you're in charge. I won't go to California."

They glanced at each other. I thought I saw Preston shrug, but I wasn't sure of it.

"We're going to give you a break," Donovan said.

His tone of voice didn't fit with his words. Break, hell! Not in the mood they were in.

"Our hands are tied here," Donovan said. "You hang around here with the heat on you, there's nothing we can do for you. In California—if you want to cooperate—maybe we can work something out."

"Work something out like what?" I said.

"Unofficial deputy," he said.

I looked at him for a long time.

"Unofficial," I said. "That means I won't get paid, huh?"

He shrugged.

"You got a client to pay the expenses. Maybe we can work something out with the D.A. here—if you come up with something."

"What would I come up with? Give me an example."

"One thing—you could come up with Barnes. I checked him out pretty good, and there's no way we can have him picked up. We don't have enough on him. He's a good lead. He had the hots for this Nick Royal's daughter, but that's no crime, unless he attacked her. But if he was so hot that he had a meeting with Royal and one thing led to another and he had Ludowicz's help, especially that big bastard—that could be our answer. And Barnes lives right here in Illinois, and nobody has told us to lay off of him."

I looked at Preston and then at Donovan, and I still couldn't really believe it, but there it was looking back at me.

"Some deal," I said. "You'll trade me for Barnes—if I bring him back."

"That's about the size of it," Preston said.

"Or," Donovan said, "you can hang around town and trot down to the station every few hours and do some explaining."

"And my client is supposed to pay for all this?"

"Like I said," Donovan said, "I'll try to work something out. You can work for your client, too."

"Sure I can."

"Why not?"

"I got one other question," I said. "Suppose Barnes didn't do it?"

"We don't expect miracles," Donovan said. "If you find out Barnes didn't do it—to our satisfaction—maybe you can find out who did. Just keep in touch."

"What if I don't want to?" I said.

"You can say yes or no, right here. If you don't want to, then you ain't going to California, if you have to sit here and starve to death for lack of work."

So all right. They were bluffing me big. But they knew that I knew what side my bread was buttered on. They knew I'd cooperate. The only real question that remained was: Could I make the flight on time?

Nothing easier. I finished packing and made sure I had all my credit cards, and they gave me a free ride to the airport with the sirens wide open all the way. The only thing Donovan said by way of farewell was, "Good luck."

* * * *

At nine the next morning, from a hotel across from the Los Angeles International Airport, I started calling Max Fisher, who was listed in an office on Wilshire Boulevard. Lawyers don't always return calls from strangers, and I kept trying every five minutes till nine thirty-five, when I finally got him.

"You are Nick Royal's lawyer?" I asked.

"Well, I was—Yes, that's right."

I introduced myself, and it didn't mean anything to him, which was all right with me "Does the name Ralph Peterson mean anything to you?" I asked him.

"I can't say it does."

"I have some reason to think he may have got in touch with Mrs. Edgar Royal, and I was hoping you could put me in touch with her."

He was firm.

"I'm afraid I can't do that without more information."

"What about Ray Barnes, a friend of Eloise Royal? Can you put me in touch with him?"

"No, I can't."

"When would it be possible to see you?"

"I'm in court this morning and probably well into the afternoon. You may call me at home after five. I'm in the book, on Coral Avenue, south of Santa Monica."

"I'll call," I said.

He hung up. I went through all the telephone directories covering the Los Angeles area and found no listing for either Edgar Royal or Gretchen. Nor was Henry Fielding listed, nor the League for Good Government.

I went to a public phone in the hotel lobby, where it would be cheaper per call, and went through the drudgery of checking out hotels for Ralph Peterson. Eighteen dollars and forty-five minutes later, I hadn't advanced a hairsbreadth. I felt badly split over the whole thing, having the double job to do. A few times I heard myself asking for Ray Barnes when I ought to have said Ralph Peterson. I didn't find a trace of either of them. I looked up Max Fisher's home number, made a note of it, then called Jackson Rivers. He was out of the office, and I had some breakfast and called him again at about ten-fifteen. He was still out.

If I could find Karl Schneider, I thought, he could lead me to Gretchen Royal, I bet.

But I don't want to see Schneider, I thought. Schneider is my favorite loser.

At eleven I got hold of Jackson Rivers, and he agreed to have lunch with me in Hollywood at noon. I drove over there, arriving twenty minutes late in a rented car. I hadn't been around Los Angeles for several years, and it seemed to me that all the streets had been changed around during my absence.

Rivers was a wiry little guy about fifty, whom I had known in Chicago when he worked for Willmark and free-lanced on the side. The first thing he said to me was: "Better learn to get along without that hat. Around here, you stick out like a dinosaur. You even smell like Chicago from a distance."

"I'll work on it," I said.

He repeated what he had wired me about Peterson's arrival at Burbank, which was all he had.

"I'll keep my eyes open," he said. "But I've got a rough schedule the next few days."

"I've got one lead," I said. "Possible only. From Mrs. Edgar Royal."

"Gretchen Royal?"

"You know her?"

"Huh-uh, but she's been in the news lately. Old Nick Royal got rubbed out, huh? Are you in on that?"

"No," I said. "Can I find out how to get to Gretchen Royal?"

He thought about it.

"Not easy," he said. "I think she lives down the coast, in Orange County. That lousy Nazi outfit Nick was mixed up in is uptight right now. The T-men have been nosing around."

"Yeah," I said.

I didn't want to talk about it.

"I maybe can get you a telephone number for her," Rivers said. "I don't know about the address. Plenty of people would know where she lives, but I don't know who those people would be."

"It wouldn't do me any good to try to talk to her on the phone," I said.

"Let me see what I can do when I get back to the office," he said. "Which, come to think of it, I better git."

I hadn't finished my lunch, and he said he'd call me at the restaurant about his try on Gretchen Royal.

"There's an eye who may be out here," I said, "who is connected to the Royal thing. Name of Karl Schneider."

"Yeah," he said. "You want to get in touch with him?"

"No, I want to not get in touch with him. I only mention it as a warning. Watch out for him."

"O.K., thanks," he said. "I'll call you."

* * * *

I was on my second cup of coffee when he called.

"The luck is not too bad," he said. "I got a phone number and address for Gretchen Royal—her own place in Newport Beach. Here are the numbers."

He gave me the numbers.

"To get there," he said, "take the San Diego Freeway and keep on south when it ends. Won't take long—forty-five minutes if you hurry."

I said goodbye to him and got started. It took quite a lot longer than forty-five minutes, but that was because it took me a long time to find the San Diego Freeway. Once I got on it, I went along at a good fast clip. And I found the house in Newport Beach with not too much backing and filling.

There wasn't anything spectacular about it, nor even prepossessing. California houses all seem to look alike until you get close and study the detail. But it was a comfortable-looking large house on a hill, overlooking the harbor from some distance. A driveway climbed up one side of the lot and disappeared in the back. In the rear, no doubt, there would be a swimming pool and patio, with an electric barbecue machine and some tables with umbrellas over them. All the shades were drawn, and the house itself appeared to be empty, lifeless.

I got out of the car, started up the front walk, then remembered what Jackson Rivers had said about my hat. I went back to the car, tossed the hat into the back seat and started off again. I felt exposed and vulnerable about the head, but I imagined one could get used to going naked from the neck up.

I rang a doorbell that jangled faintly inside the house, then waited a few minutes. After a while I rang it again, and the door opened. There was a maid in a white dress, drying her hands on a paper towel.

"Is Mrs. Royal in?" I asked.

She shook her head.

"No. She's not."

"When do you expect her?"

"I just don't know. She didn't say when to expect her."

"All right," I said, "thanks very much."

She nodded and pushed the door shut. I went back to the car and sat there. Looking down the hill, beyond the Coast Highway, I could see what looked like several thousand boats in slips along the harbor front. Some were impressively large and expensive-looking, and there were quite a few small delicate shells of boats that would be tricky, I thought, on the open sea. There was a steady flow of cars on the Coast Highway in both directions, and there were a few boats drifting around the harbor. There was hardly a soul anywhere on foot. The California sun glanced off the shiny parts of the boats and off the water and glared through my windshield. I wished I had remembered to buy sunglasses.

I had sat there for about ten minutes when Eloise Royal came out of the house and down the front walk. She was wearing shorts and a halter and sunglasses. She was barefoot. There was no place for me to go. I sat there, waiting for her to turn and go down the hill toward the beach, but she didn't turn. She stood on the curb for a while, then stepped into the street and walked across toward my car. Six feet away, she stopped and then she came on, folded her arms on the windowsill, put her chin on the top arm and said, "What do you want now? When did you come to California?"

I couldn't think of anything to say right off. It was disconcerting to try to look at her through her glasses, which were so dark they were almost black. Her eyes were only darker shadows in her skull.

"I wanted to talk to your mother for a minute," I said.

"About me?"

"No, not about you."

"About my father?"

"No."

"My father's dead, you know."

"Yes, I know."

She hung there by her chin, and as far as I could tell, she was staring at me steadily. But the glasses made it deceptive. I couldn't be sure.

"How come you're not wearing your hat?" she said.

"Well, I thought—people in California don't wear hats. When in Rome."

"What?"

"When in Rome, do as the Romans do. It's an old saying."

"I know it," she said. "What does it mean?"

"It means you follow the customs of the country, whatever they may be, if you want to stay out of trouble."

"Are you in trouble?"

"Not that I know of."

"If you stay here much longer, you'll be in trouble."

"I will?"

"The cops don't like people hanging around in their cars—around places like this."

"What places?"

"Nice places. Neighborhoods."

"I see," I said.

"As long as I'm here talking to you it's all right," she said. "But what if I go away?"

"Then maybe you'll stay here and talk to me."

"Huh-uh. Ray Barnes is coming to get me."

"Oh?" I said.

"We're going to Wil Wright's, and then I don't know where."

"What's Wil Wright's?"

"It's an ice cream place. You know."

"It sounds good."

"It's pretty good."

"What does your mother think about Ray Barnes?"

The simple-little-girl put-on she was giving me was getting under my skin.

"My mother doesn't care what I do," she said, "as long as I don't run away."

"Well, it could be a nuisance to her to have to go looking for you."

"That's not it," she said. "It's all about money. If I don't live with her, she doesn't get the money from my father's will."

"It would seem to me that's your money."

"Not till I'm twenty-one."

"I see."

"Anyway it's not real."

"Not real money?"

"I mean the whole thing. Nothing is real."

"Oh," I said. And after a minute I said, "Are the boats real?"

She looked down toward the harbor.

"No," she said.

She looked at me again—perhaps.

"Are you going to try to break it up between me and Ray Barnes?" she asked.

"Of course not," I said.

"That's why you're here, isn't it? My mother sent for you to keep me away from Ray Barnes."

"No," I said. "I don't have any interest in you and Ray Barnes."

"You have an interest in my mother?"

"I just want some information from her."

"About me?"

"That's where we started, isn't it? All the way around now."

"I don't believe you," she said.

"O.K.," I said.

She straightened lazily and pushed herself back from the door.

"Are you real?" she said.

"The last time I checked," I said, "I was real."

"How can you tell?"

"There are signs. I can tell."

She looked at the harbor again for a while.

"My mother won't be back for a long time," she said. "She went to have lunch with…somebody. Mr. Fielding won't like it."

"Mr. Fielding won't like it?"

"He sure won't."

"Is Mr. Fielding real?" I asked.

The black sunglasses gazed at me blankly.

"My father was real," she said.

She turned away and walked back toward the house, her miniature behind doing its best to waggle in the tight shorts. No sooner had she disappeared inside than a car pulled up in front of the house and Ray Barnes got out of it. He glanced across at me but apparently failed to recognize me and went up to the front door.

Maybe Jackson Rivers had something after all, about the hat, I thought.

I wanted very much not to have an altercation with Ray Barnes on the public streets, and I was fairly certain Eloise would tell him about me, so I pulled ahead slowly, found a place to turn around and drove back up the street past the house. I made two or three turns, and when I got within sight of Gretchen Royal's house again, Barnes' car was gone. I pulled into the curb, and I had sat there for maybe three or four minutes when a black and white police car drifted past me. It stopped and backed up slowly, and the officer on the near side of the front seat looked at me for a while.

The little monkey turned me in, I thought.

"Waiting for someone?" the officer said.

"Yes," I said.

He looked at me some more.

"This is a school zone," he said. "You'll have to move on."

I looked along the street.

"School zone?" I said.

"The school's around the corner," he said.

"I didn't realize school was in session."

He was looking at me in a new way now, the hard, meaningful way a cop learns to look at people.

"Summer school," he said.

I knew that if I held out any longer, he would start checking out my ID and one thing and another and make life mildly miserable for a while and in general interfere with my work. So I started the car and rolled ahead while they waited. I drove to the Coast Highway and turned south, and they followed me for several blocks and finally turned off. I pulled up in front of a restaurant and cocktail lounge called the Surfer and went in to get a drink.

It was getting along toward four o'clock. I couldn't figure out how long I ought to wait around for Gretchen Royal. I was going on the slender lead that if Ralph Peterson had come out to see Nick Royal, it would be natural for him to look up the nearest person to him, if he couldn't find him otherwise, or if he knew Nick was dead. No reason for Gretchen to hold out. But Eloise's remarks had made me nervous about it. There was a strong likelihood that Gretchen wouldn't know anything about Ralph Peterson at all, and I would have wasted the afternoon—Mrs. Peterson's afternoon.

The public telephone was in the men's room, which made it nice and private. I arranged with the operator to charge the call to my hotel room and placed it person to person to Mrs. Ralph Peterson in Chicago.

Her voice lifted when I told her who was calling, then fell when I said, "Nothing yet, sorry."

"I see," she said. "Well—"

"Have you ever visited California with your husband?" I asked.

"Several times."

"Did you have a favorite hotel, or other place to stay during your visits?"

"Yes. Every time but one, I think, we stayed at the Beverly Hills Hotel."

"All right, thanks." I knew for sure I had checked out the Beverly Hills Hotel, and Peterson had not been registered under his own name.

"Another thing may help, if you have the names of any friends out here, special friends, your husband's or mutual friends. He might have got in touch with some of them."

"Yes, he might," she said. But she said it wistfully, without real hope.

"If I could have their names and addresses—"

"Of course, but it will take a little while. I'm no good remembering things like that—"

"Then could you do this? List them for me and put it in a telegram, to me at the International Hotel, Los Angeles. I'll get it in a couple of hours then."

"Yes, I will. I'll do that." A pause, and then, "Do you have any idea at all—"

"I don't have anything specific," I said. "But I'll keep at it."

"I feel, somehow, so kind of prying and suspicious," she said, "checking up on him like this—"

"Do you want me to stop?"

A longer pause.

"No," she said finally, firming up. "I have to know. I have to know."

"All right, I'll call again soon."

"Please do," she said.

I made a note to remind myself to recheck the Beverly Hills Hotel, and when I got back to my barstool, Karl Schneider was sitting two stools away.

CHAPTER 11

I finished my highball, and he worked on his. Neither of us said a word for about five minutes. Then Schneider said, "Small world."

There wasn't anything in the book to say to that. I ordered another drink. I was damned if I'd let him get me running, though I felt like running.

"Don't get your hopes up," I said.

"O.K., tough guy," he said.

"Watch it," I said.

"Uh-huh. I understand you checked out a couple of Barnes' hired goons."

"I was doing it for a friend," I said. "I guess nothing came of it."

"Maybe a little. I found out Nick Royal paid a visit to Barnes in Chicago."

I blinked.

"At the Palmer House?"

"How do you like that?"

"Number one," I said, "I don't believe it. Number two, if it's true, I don't care. O.K.?"

"O.K.," he said. And pretty soon he said, "I bet Lieutenant Donovan would like to know."

How did he get onto that? I wondered.

I shrugged.

"He's pretty good," I said. "He can do his own hunting."

"All right," he said. "I got the message."

He tossed off the rest of his highball, got down from the stool and left the joint. I stayed where I was, feeling superior and relieved, which is quite a trick when you do them simultaneously.

I took my time finishing the drink, made a firm decision to drive to the Beverly Hills Hotel and left the bar at four forty-one. Schneider was nowhere in sight. I felt relieved and not quite so superior.

* * * *

It was after six when I got to the big hotel on Sunset Boulevard, and it was a bad time to arrive. Traffic was stacked up on the narrow drive leading to the entrance and the doorman just laughed at the $5 bill I showed when I said, "I may need it in a hurry."

"No way," he said. "We'll park it as close as possible, but that ain't very close."

I gave up the car and went into the main lobby, where at least a hundred people were congregated. I had heard that you could always find a seat in the Polo Lounge, but they had broken the rule this day. I wandered around for a while, peering at faces, finding none of any interest. By way of routine I asked at the desk for Mr. Ralph Peterson, and the clerk said they had no Ralph Peterson registered. I finally found a vacant seat in an undesirable location in the vast lobby and settled myself in it. I couldn't see much except the main entrance and the entrance to the main dining room, where patrons were already beginning to arrive.

They came in all sizes, colors and styles from chic to gaudy and from vivid to drab. There were a lot of miniskirts of an extremeness seldom to be seen east of the Sunset Strip. Sprinkled here and there were a few types who would be equally at home in Pasadena society, but they were rarities. None of the men I looked at bore any resemblance to Ralph Peterson as I had contrived from photo and description to picture him.

Unlike most assignments of this kind, the grind of sitting in one place, watching, was less tedious than it might have been. The spectacle was continual and colorful, and it changed enough to be exciting. Still, after nearly an hour of futile observation, I was restless. The lobby crowd had thinned, and there were other chairs available, so I got up and stretched my legs. There were telephones along a shelf in a hall just off the main lobby, and some of them faced the desk and the front door. I put some money in one of them, dialed my hotel at the airport and asked for any messages. There was a telephone message from Lieutenant Donovan in Chicago. There was also a lengthy telegram from Chicago, and I asked the operator to find a public stenographer who would read it to me and stand by. She said it would take a few minutes, so I hung up and waited at the phone for her to call back. It took about ten minutes, and I watched the lobby steadily, without seeing anyone who might have been Peterson.

The phone rang, and it was the stenographer, who said she had the telegram, which was from a Naomi Peterson in Chicago and was mostly two lists of names and addresses. One list was headed "Ralph," and the other "Mutual." I got out a notebook and pencil and asked her to read me the names, starting with the Ralphs.

There were seven names, and they all had telephone numbers except one. I asked her to read the other list, which was shorter—only five names, and two of them lacked telephone numbers.

"No other message?" I asked.

"It says, 'Good luck.' That's all," she said.

"O.K., thanks," I said and hung up.

I went to the desk to get change and returned to the telephone. I was still watching the lobby, but with little more than simple curiosity by now. I started down the list of Ralph Peterson's California friends. A man answered the first call—a man named Jackson—and I introduced myself as a friend of Peterson's.

"Yeah. Well, he's in Chicago as far as I know."

"I'd heard he planned to come out here for a few days," I said.

"I don't know, I haven't heard from him."

"All right," I said. "Thanks."

The next try gave the same results with minor variations. I was on the third one, letting it ring at the other end, when Gretchen Royal appeared in the hall, coming straight at me. Her preoccupation and the fact that I wasn't wearing my hat saved both of us from the shock of recognition. I turned, not too hurriedly, so that my elbow rested on the shelf, and she passed me and went to one of the house phones on another shelf behind me. Another break I got was that it appeared nobody was home at the number I was calling, so I could let it ring and not have to get involved in conversation. With my free ear, I heard Gretchen speak into a house phone.

"Bungalow nine," she said, and waited a few seconds. Then, "Hello, it's me... Yes, it was all right, but I only found a few of the things I wanted... Listen, I can't stay for dinner; I just don't dare, not tonight... My darling daughter is in a real snit, and I can't take a chance—she knows we had lunch today... Yes, all right, I'll have one drink... Yes, right away."

She hung up. I stood there till she had disappeared, hung up on the no-answer number and moved away from the phones. I stood around for three or four minutes, and a bellboy came along.

"How do I get to Bungalow Nine?" I asked him.

"Out here," he said, pointing, "first turn left, second on the right."

I went outside, where the bungalows are scattered on the big lawn like flowers, the California trees fragrant in the summer evening. Lights shone in them like fireflies. I took the first left turn, strolling, passed Bungalow 8 and then 9 and went on to a dark area where I could loiter.

I didn't have to loiter long. After not more than five minutes, the door opened and Gretchen came out, followed by a man in a dark sport shirt and summer slacks. There was little to be seen of him at my distance. He didn't look like anyone I had ever seen before.

They went down to the main walk together and stood for a minute. Gretchen lifted her face, the man kissed her once, and she walked away without looking back. He watched till she had disappeared; then he returned to the bungalow. I counted to five slowly and went down there.

The door opened almost at once. He seemed surprised to see me, but he didn't seem distressed. The light was not too good, being mostly behind him, but his dark hair and the shape of his face made him a strong likelihood.

"Yes?" he said.

"Ralph Peterson?" I said. "From Chicago?"

Sometimes it works; sometimes it doesn't. If you hit them with their real identity without warning, sometimes the reflex will work for you. In this case it worked, but it took a few seconds.

"Who's asking?" he said.

"I'm from Chicago," I said. "Your wife is concerned about you. I've been looking for you. That's all."

He gazed at something beyond my head, and finally he came across with it.

"Yes, I'm Ralph Peterson," he said. "I'm flying home tomorrow. I'm sorry my wife was concerned. Should have let her know, but—"

"You came out here to see Nick Royal?" I said.

"How did you know?"

"I had some background on you. Just put a couple of things together."

"That's correct," he said. "Nick and I are old war buddies. He wrote me that he needed some help, and on the spur of the moment I flew out here. After I got here, I found he had been killed, in Chicago. So I looked up his wife—ex-wife—to see whether there was anything I could do. And there wasn't."

"You don't have to explain to me," I said. "But thanks for making it easy. You might give your wife a ring. I'll report that you're on your way home."

"All right," he said. "Good night."

"Good night," I said.

He closed the door firmly, as he should have. Everything was done. Whatever he had with Gretchen Royal was no part of my assignment. I went back to the hotel lobby and used one of the telephones to send a telegram to Mrs. Peterson. It read: "Ralph Peterson flying home tomorrow."

I wanted to add some words of comfort and advice but decided against it. Those paternalistic impulses only get you in trouble.

I went to the Polo Lounge and bought a long cool drink, and after a while I went outside, sent for my car and drove back to the International Hotel. From my room I put in a call to Donovan and finally got to him.

"Listen," he growled, "we got descriptions of the two that worked over Schneider in that bar. Take 'em down."

"Hold it! What for?"

"Take 'em down!"

I found a pencil.

"Donovan," I said, "all I'm supposed to do is to pick up Barnes—"

"Just take the goddam descriptions."

Of course, I would take the descriptions. I would always do what Donovan ordered. That was how I had been taught my trade.

"Those are the two muscles I told you about," I said after he had read the descriptions. "What do you want me to do about it?"

"Look for them!"

"Where did you get these?"

"From the bartender at the Duckblind joint."

"Did he clear me?"

A pause.

"Hell, no. How could he do that?"

"You still want Barnes?"

"You're damn right. Because we got the same descriptions from Mr. Ludwig, and he was working for Barnes. Good luck."

He hung up. He wasn't having any arguments. He had got me to California on a threat. But things had changed now. He could no longer make the threat stick. But he had a better thing, a simpler thing. *You be nice to me and I will be nice to you.* There were a lot of years behind it. A lot of close, rugged years.

Someone was knocking on my door, a small insistent knocking. I went over and opened the door, and Eloise Royal threw herself at me.

CHAPTER 12

Her little hands and wrists were clammy on the back of my neck. She was shaking so hard I could hear her teeth knock together. She smelled of salt and sweat. Her long hair was snarled and damp. She made sounds against my chest, but they weren't real words.

I carried her to the couch, covered her with my jacket, drew some hot water from the tap in the bathroom and brought it back. She wouldn't have anything to do with it for a long time, but finally when I held her up, holding tight with one arm, and put it to her mouth, she drank some. She was still shaking.

"You got to do something…" she said, her teeth chattering. "Please… do something—"

"Easy," I said. "Talk to me slow."

I made her drink some more of the hot water.

"How did you know where I am?" I asked her.

"He told me…Ray…Ray Barnes."

It seemed unlikely, but then, he was a grown man, capable of checking such places as car rental agencies and things like that. He might even have some California edition of Mr. Ludwig looking out for him.

"You've been with Barnes all this time?" I asked.

"I…had to run…I think…they did bad things to him…I think they killed him."

The atmosphere changed.

"Where?" I said.

"In that place…that…out on the beach…where he took me—"

"Could you find it?"

"Yes…sure, I know where it is."

"Can you tell me where it is?"

"It's out by the beach…It's his mother's house."

That told me.

"How did you get here?" I asked her.

"In a taxi…but I had to walk a long time to get one. The taxi driver helped me find your room."

"Do you have any idea where Karl Schneider is?"

She put her tight fist in her mouth.

"Oh, God," she said, "don't start that again."

Her shaking had diminished, and she lay still, gazing wide-eyed at the ceiling, chewing her fist.

"If you can tell me where the place is," I said, "I'll call the police right away—"

"No, not the police."

"They can get there sooner than I can."

"No," she said. "It's not far, just down by the beach—"

"Near your mother's house?"

"No, up here, Venice, not far."

She turned suddenly, and the couch lurched under her. She took her hand out of her mouth and put it on my face.

"Mac—please? I know I acted shitty to you—I'm sorry. I don't know where to go!"

"How are you feeling? Are you very cold?"

"No, I'm all right."

"All right," I said. "Show me where it is."

She was dizzy when she got up, but she stood all right after I steadied her. I got my sweater out of the suitcase and made her put it on. The sleeves were eight inches too long, and her shoulders could have fit it twice; but it would keep her warm.

Going down to the parking entrance, I couldn't help thinking of Ralph Peterson.

Like mother, like daughter? I thought.

But there was little to do but check it out. She lived in at least two worlds, and one of them was surely real.

In the car, as I pulled out of the lot, she was fairly calm.

"You have to go to Lincoln," she said, "and just keep going, to Washington."

"How do I get to Lincoln?"

"By—well—you turn on Sepulveda—right up there."

So she knew where she was when she had to.

"Will you tell me what happened, with you and Barnes?"

I made the turn on Sepulveda all right.

"We went to Wil Wright's," she said, "and I had a hot fudge sundae. I don't remember what Ray had—"

"I don't need every detail," I said. "Mainly, how did you come to go to this house, and what happened after you got there?"

"Well, we were talking about things, and I was talking about how things were around the house and how funny my mother was acting and I hate the whole scene anyway, and Ray said he would take me to his mother's house, where he was staying, and we could have dinner and talk some more. He said we would call my mother and tell her where I was, and then he would take me home, or somewhere else, if I didn't want to go home."

"Did he say whether his mother was also at the house?"

"No. She wasn't there—she's on a trip—but he didn't mention about that."

"Where were some of the other places he might have taken you, if you hadn't wanted to go home?"

"We talked about that—about my father's lawyer, Mr. Fisher, and about a boardinghouse at the college that he knew about—"

"Where did you live, by the way, at the college?"

"In a dorm. I hated it."

"All right, so you were talking, and then—"

"Well, I was beginning to get scared, the way he was talking—"

"Barnes?"

"Yeah, he talked funny. He started asking me questions—personal-type questions—and he would ask me if I loved him and stuff like that—"

"Was he unpleasant about it?"

"Well, you know, it was like talking to a doctor or something."

"And you didn't go for this talk?"

"It made me feel funny. That's all. I don't mean he said anything really dirty or anything, but—"

"O.K. Now when did the people come in? When did the bad things start?"

We were winding down a long hill between open fields, and the only lights were at a distance. The land ahead was flat.

"You have to turn pretty soon," she said.

"Left or right?"

"Uh, left."

"You were saying?" I said.

"Yeah, I finally told him I didn't want to talk about that stuff anymore, and we went for a walk along the beach. And when we got back to the house, the two guys were sitting there, in the living room."

"Two guys? Did you know them? Did Barnes know them?"

"They're guys that work for Uncle Edgar and Mr. Fielding. They used to work for my father."

"What did they say they wanted?"

"They wanted me to go with them."

"Go where?"

"Home. They said my mother sent them to get me."

"Did you believe them?"

"Oh, I guess so. Why not? But I said I wouldn't go. And they said I would have to go with them, and Ray got very angry and started yelling at them."

"What did they do then?"

"They started hitting him. They knocked his glasses off and pushed him down and one of them started kicking him in the ribs, and…that's when I ran."

We came to what seemed to be the end of the boulevard, and there were rows of beach houses and shacks and a few stores, cramped-looking with no open space between them.

"Left or right?" I asked.

"Right," she said. "It's about—it's up the beach a ways."

"You got out of there, and they were beating up Ray, is that it?"

"Yes. I didn't know what else to do."

That's all right, I was thinking, but I wonder why they manage to let her get away all the time?

"Slow down now," she said, "it's right in here someplace—" The neighborhood was old and very dingy. There were narrow streets leading off the main street at close intervals, but some of them weren't streets at all, but only wide walkways with iron rails to keep you from driving into them. Every other real street was marked one way, with the arrow against you.

"Slow," she said, leaning forward and moving a finger as if counting. "It's the next one I think up there—" I slowed and finally turned left at the first possibility. It was more an alley than a street, with the houses backed up to it on both sides, and dead ahead, only a scant block away, was the beach. It was very dark down there, except for periodic lights along a wide beach walk.

"Where will I be able to leave the car?" I asked.

"I don't know. You just have to find a place."

That seemed impossible. Space was what Venice was entirely out of. Cars were parked tightly against the backs of the old houses, and there were signs at each place reading NO PARKING—CARS WILL BE TOWED AWAY.

I came up behind an old hotel that looked as if it had been abandoned for years, except that there were some lights in it. A narrow drive led off the alley into a parking area. There were a few open slots, and I headed into one.

"You can't park here," she said, "it's for the hotel—"

"It looks as if I have to park here."

"All right," she said.

I helped her out of the car, and she hiked the long sweater sleeves up on her arms. The ocean smell was very strong. There was a stiff breeze blowing, and the beach appeared to be deserted.

"It's the one over there," she said, pointing.

A sizable frame house with a peaked roof sat somewhat by itself across from the hotel. Its front yard was the beach sand, and in back, enclosed by a high wooden fence, were a garage and parking area. A gate was open in the fence, and a car stood in the drive, its back end projecting into the alley.

"Is that Barnes' car?" I asked.

"I think so. Yes," she said.

There were no other cars nearby, and nobody loitering in the vicinity.

"I want you to stay close to me," I said, "and do exactly what I tell you right away, even if it sounds funny. O.K.?"

She slipped one hand under my right arm.

"O.K.," she said.

I looked into the parked car, and it was empty. There was a back door, but it was dark and narrow and looked like a bad entrance. I led her along the alley and around to the front of the place, where a low-roofed porch over-looked the beach. There was a light inside the house, and the front door was closed. We went up one step, and I looked into the window. The shade was drawn; but there were cracks at both sides, and I could see slantwise into a square living room, over-furnished with early Grand Rapids odds and ends. The light came from a high globular lamp with a green shade. I couldn't see any sign of life.

"Is he there?" she asked, huddling against me. "Is Ray there?"

"I can't tell," I said. "Stay behind me now, and if I say, 'Run,' you run back to the car and lock yourself in."

"All right," she said.

I opened a screen, tried the knob of the front door and found it locked. But the door was loose, and light showed through the slit between door and jamb. I put my shoulder to it, lifted on the knob and gave it a try. It only took two tries to force it open.

I paused on the threshold, waiting, feeling Eloise pressing into my back. The house smelled damp and moldy. I looked around the door and saw that a chair had been tipped over. A spilling ashtray lay near it on the floor, and the contents of an overturned suitcase were strewn here and there.

I pushed the door wide and walked two strides into the room, and a guy came from the back of the house, from the dark into the light. Eloise's face nudged my shoulder blades when I stopped.

"Hello again," Karl Schneider said. "Come in. Make yourself at home."

CHAPTER 13

There was a sudden absence of Eloise behind me. I turned, and she was backing off toward a corner of the room, her eyes intent on Schneider.

"Where is he?" she said. "Where did you—What did you do with him?"

"It's all right, kid," he said. "They took him to the hospital."

"What hospital?"

"I don't know. He'll live. They were taking him away when I got here. The neighbors were out. 'Who is it?' I said. 'Man named Barnes,' somebody said. 'His mother owns the house.' Somebody else said, 'He had a little girl with him.' 'What happened to her?' I asked. But nobody knew. 'There was some kind of a big fight,' somebody said. And they put Barnes in the wagon and drove away. There were some cops, but they didn't stay long."

"I want to know where he is," Eloise said.

"I'll try to find out," Schneider said.

She stood stone-still, huddled into the corner, until she seemed to become a part of the house. She was dark in the sweater and skirt and stockings. Only her white face and hands seemed real. Or unreal.

"How did you find your way here?" I asked Schneider. He shrugged.

"I knew where Barnes was staying; I followed him here from the airport. I lost him this afternoon after he left Wil Wright's with Eloise; I'd lost them when I saw you in that bar in Newport. I didn't think they came here, because they were traveling south when I lost them. I finally came over here."

"I guess you were lucky to miss the party," I said.

"I don't know," he said. "I'd like to get my hands on them—if it was the same guys."

I looked at Eloise.

"Was it the same guys," I asked, "the ones that beat up Karl in Chicago?"

She moved her face away.

"Yes," she said, "the same."

"Why wouldn't you identify them in Chicago?"

"Because…" she said. "I didn't know you. I didn't know what was happening. I was scared."

I looked around at the mess on the floor and smelled the rank ocean smell and looked at Eloise in the corner, and it seemed to me there was nothing that could be done that I would know anything about.

"Eloise," I said, "if it were up to you altogether, no problems—where would you want to go?"

She gazed at me out of the dark little eyes in her white face enclosed in all the hair. Her mouth moved a little, and then she sank slowly downward, like a series of stroboscopic films of a wilting flower, till she was all the way on the floor with her face in her arms.

"I don't know," she said. "I don't know. There's no place—"

I went over there and knelt and touched her, then got my arms under her and lifted. Schneider was leaning over close by, watching. I looked at him. He still had the gargoyle look, but most of his bruises had softened.

"Max Fisher?" I said.

"I guess so," he said.

"You know where his place is?"

"Yeah."

I got on my feet with her, and we went outside. In the short time since we had gone into the house, a fog had come in, and gray swaths of it were swirling above the beach.

"I came in a cab," Schneider said. "My car's at Max Fisher's house."

"You've talked to him?"

"Uh-huh. Not much to be done."

We crossed over to the hotel parking lot, and he opened the rear door of the car for me.

"You know where it is," I said. "You drive, all right?"

"Sure."

I got her into the back seat, stretched her out and held her while Schneider got the thing started. She was limp at first, and then she curled her legs and put her face in my arm. Schneider worked his way through the tight alleys onto the main street without too much trouble and drove back in the direction from which Eloise and I had come to the Barnes house. I didn't pay too much attention, being preoccupied with thoughts of Eloise and once in a while—unhappily—Lieutenant Donovan of the Chicago police.

It was a short trip, and we arrived unexpectedly to me. The fog was thickening when we pulled up on a beach street at the end of a row of imposing houses, most of which were dark. Sand was piled in random dunes between them. In Max Fisher's house lights glowed remotely through drawn blinds. A black Mercedes was parked on a wide drive to the right of the house, and a light-colored Chevrolet had been parked at the curb.

Eloise hadn't spoken a word during the ride, but when Schneider opened the door and I lifted her, trying to help her out, she hung onto me with both hands and said, "Tell Max Fisher to find out where Ray is."

"All right," I said.

"Promise?" she said.

"I promise."

When we got out, I started to lift her again, but she pulled away.

"I can walk all right," she said.

The front door was recessed in a half-screened entry, filled with planters sprouting exotic-looking plants. We were passing, three abreast, when an entry light went on suddenly and the front door opened. The man who had opened stood square in the doorway, looking at us. He was stocky, but trim, in a costly black suit and white shirt, and he had black crew-cut hair.

"Hello, Max," Eloise said.

He didn't say anything. He looked tight and tense, as if he didn't trust himself to say anything. He was looking at me.

"This is Mac," Schneider said. "He's the one they pulled Nick Royal's body off of."

Some introduction.

Fisher shifted his eyes to Eloise and said, "All right, come in. But don't settle down."

We followed him up two steps and into a big living room with windows overlooking the beach. But there was nothing out there now but fog.

"Where did you find her?" Fisher asked.

"Up in Venice," Schneider said. "Well, it was really Mac who found her."

"No," I said, "she found me."

Fisher looked impatient. Eloise just stood with her hands at her sides, staring into space. Fisher turned on her with some exasperation.

"Eloise, listen to me," he said. "Your mother is your legal custodian. In about a year from now you'll be eighteen. By that time your father's will can be settled in probate. There will be some money for you. But until that time you don't have any choice. You'll have to live with your mother."

She stood mute. Fisher was a good, forceful man, but not much of a match for her stubbornness.

"Your mother was here in this house for about two hours, while we wondered where you were," he said. "I made a deal with her. I told her that as soon as you were found, I would see to it that you were brought home. That's what's going to happen now." He looked at Schneider. "And I will appreciate a little help from one or both of you, in case it should be necessary."

Eloise's mouth twitched maliciously. It was the first thing resembling a smile I had ever seen on her face. She looked at me.

"You promised," she said.

"Yeah," I said. "Mr. Fisher, it would be a kindness to Eloise if you would find out where they took Ray Barnes."

His mouth opened, and he shook his head slightly. Schneider told him Barnes had been taken to some hospital.

"Well, all right," Fisher said. "I'll try. Now we'd better get started."

Eloise stood her ground.

"Not till you find out where Ray is," she said.

"Listen, at this hour of the night—"

"I don't care," she said. "Find out."

His mouth tightened in refusal.

"Then I won't go," she said, backing off. "I'll kick and scream. I'll wake up the neighbors. I'll break everything in your goddam house!"

Uneven footsteps sounded outside the open front door. Fisher started over there. He looked out the door, stopped and retreated slowly into the room. A guy came in, very slowly, supporting himself with one hand against the doorjamb. The other hand was in a sling. He was Ray Barnes, and he was in sorry shape. One eye was completely shut and swollen blue. There were cuts on his face. The arm in the sling he held tightly against his chest, where, I could guess, there was about half a mile of tightly bound adhesive tape. Eloise stared at him, started toward him and stopped.

"Don't fight it anymore, Eloise," Barnes said. "Go back to your mother. They're too tough for us. I can't help you now."

"Ray—" She put out a hand, but he didn't accept it.

"I was crazy," he said. "I flipped a little. It took those two to knock some sense into me—anyway, some reality. You go home now. I'll write to you."

He turned and went out the way he had come. Eloise didn't try to follow him.

Fisher snapped off one of the brighter inside lights.

"Let's get started," he said. "It's a long trip."

"To Newport?" Eloise said.

"No. Mr. Fielding's house."

"Oh, God," she said.

I helped her down the front steps, and Schneider followed. I heard Fisher close the door behind him and come after us. Across the street Barnes was climbing carefully into a taxi. Fisher was heading for the Mercedes. I looked at Schneider, and we cut away and walked over to the cab. Eloise stood in the street. Schneider and I looked in the open window at Ray Barnes.

"How you feeling?" I asked.

"I'll be all right," he said. "They said I would be all right."

He blinked at us. Without his glasses, he looked oddly exposed. Footsteps sounded, and Max Fisher was standing near Schneider, listening.

"There's something I'd like to know, if you'll tell me," I said.

"If I can," he said.

"You had a meeting with Nick Royal in Chicago. What happened there?"

"Well...Nick Royal came to see me at the Palmer House...afternoon—" He was breathing shortly, to save his ribs, and it was hard for him to talk.

"He said he wanted Eloise to continue in school, and he wanted to know there would be someone responsible looking after her. He was...checking me out—is that the word?"

"He didn't want you to stay away from her?"

"Oh, no. He didn't have any idea I was...stricken with her—any of that. He came to me because I had written him about Eloise...and he wanted to see me about it."

"Did he give any reason for wanting someone to look after her?"

"Yes...he said...it was something about this Fascist group he worked for... He said he'd been with it long enough to find out it was—a bunch of crap, he called it—and he thought he had found a way to wreck it. And he said...it was rough work and something might happen to him."

"Did he say what might happen?"

"No. I don't know whether he actually expected to get killed—"

"Did he say anything to you about Karl Schneider, in connection with Eloise?"

He moved his face to look at Schneider.

"Yes...yes, he did. He said...Schneider was the only man in the world he could trust, and he would ask him to look after her, too. He spoke very highly of Schneider."

He was breathing in gasps now, and I let him loose.

"Thanks," I said. "Take care of yourself."

He nodded and mumbled something to the driver. We stood off while the cab pulled away, and then I found Eloise, took her arm and led her over to Max Fisher's car. I got in the back seat with her, and Schneider rode in front with Fisher.

I didn't rise all the way to the drive. It was after midnight when we started, Eloise wasn't saying anything to anyone, and I was sleepy. I would doze off and wake up, and even awake, I didn't have any idea where we were, so it didn't mean much. The Mercedes made quite a lot of noise, and that added to the grind. I was grateful for the occasional sleep. We had been on the road for about an hour and a half when I woke and felt shaking and found Eloise with her face against my arm, crying. I couldn't hear her cry, but I could feel it, like miniature shock waves, vibrating against me. I put my arm around her and held her, and she cried for quite a while, all the way through a beach-side city that stretched for several miles along the ocean side of the freeway. We were coming out of it into the country again when she straightened up and got the hair out of her face.

"Who killed my father?" she said without warning.

"I don't know."

"Yes, you do. I think you do."

"I really don't. What do you think?"

"Mr. Fielding," she said.

"Mr. Fielding?"

"He hated my father. He was jealous of him because of my mother and how popular he was with the men and all that."

"But your mother is married to your Uncle Edgar."

"That doesn't mean anything. That's not real. It was my father Mr. Fielding really hated."

I gave it some thought, not much.

"You think Mr. Fielding did it with his own hands?" I said.

"No. Mr. Fielding never does anything with his own hands—except maybe to my mother—"

"Then he must have got somebody to do it for him." We were on open highway now, with broad lanes curving down along the beach. The white surf showed among patches of gray fog.

"It's not far now," she said.

We passed an odd-looking structure on the beach side of the road. A sign read CORINTH STABLES.

"Stables on the beach?" I asked.

"Sure," Eloise said. "They work the horses out in the surf. It strengthens their legs."

"Are the horses real?" I said.

After a while she said, very softly, "Yes, the horses are real. The horses are the only real thing around here."

The car slowed suddenly, swerved and made a turn onto a side road marked CASTELNUOVO—PRIVATE ROAD. We began to climb sharply, winding up into hills.

"The horses," she said, "are very real."

At the summit of the climb, we poised a moment, looking down into a deep arroyo that ran under the highway toward the beach. At its upper, inland end the ground was level, and there were lights among tall trees.

"That's Mr. Fielding's house," she said.

We started down the winding road toward the lights.

"Are you going to arrest Mr. Fielding?" she said. "For murdering my father?"

"I don't think so," I said. "I don't have any proof, and it wouldn't be legal to arrest him."

"Oh," she said. "Then I won't say anything to anybody about it."

"Thanks," I said.

She put her small hand in mine on the seat and squeezed it lightly.

"You were good to me," she said. "Thanks."

I squeezed her hand.

"You hang on," I said. "Everything will work out."

She didn't say anything to that. She was wiser than that.

We were close now. I saw hedges of the high trees. There were several buildings, some lighted, scattered among the trees and one main house fronting on the upper edge of the arroyo with a view of the beach. A drive led to the rear of the house, ending at a closed four-car garage. A dim light glowed over a passage beside the garage, leading toward the house.

Max Fisher got out of the car, opened the door for Eloise and reached in to help her out. I gave her a light push, and she went along all right. Schneider sat where he was.

Fisher and Eloise were approaching the lighted passage when a bright flashlight beam stopped them. There was a man holding the flashlight, but I couldn't make him out.

"Please tell Mrs. Royal I've brought Eloise," Fisher said.

"She'll be here in a minute," a voice said.

A second man joined the first, and the flashlight went off. After a minute I could see them in white sport shirts, one dark and heavyset, the other rangy—age twenty-nine, yellow hair, I thought. Schneider was sitting quietly in his seat, watching them through the windshield.

"Is that them?" he said pretty soon.

"It's very likely," I said.

We didn't say anything more. Rapid footsteps sounded in the passage, and Gretchen Royal, in slacks and a sweater, came into the light. Edgar Royal followed her, his glasses shining in the half-dark. I remembered his sharp, unmoving eyes.

"Go in the house," Gretchen said to Eloise, who lowered her head and went past her and Edgar into the passage and disappeared. Edgar and Gretchen said something to Max Fisher. I couldn't hear the words. After a minute Gretchen turned and disappeared, and Edgar and Max Fisher followed her.

The two with the flashlight drifted toward the car and finally came close enough to look in at us from a few feet off.

"You're with Fisher?" the dark one said.

We didn't say anything. The flash beam came on again, first long and steady in Schneider's face, then long and steady in mine. Finally, it went off.

They said something in low voices, and one of them chuckled. I looked in another direction and yawned.

Jesus, I thought, the long drive back—and another one to my hotel. I thought of Ralph Peterson, and Naomi, his wife.

I thought of Donovan and forced myself to think of something else.

Fisher came back quickly, brushed past the two of them and got into the car.

"Good night, Mr. Fisher," they said in unison.

Fisher didn't pay any attention. He backed the car, turned and headed up the private road, going a little faster than was safe. I stayed with it till we got to the highway, then curled up on the back seat and went to sleep. I didn't wake up till we pulled up at Fisher's garage. The fog was thick now, obscuring the lights inside the house. Schneider got out, and then I got out. Fisher was locking the car.

"Thanks for going along," he said. "I'll see you get paid for the time."

I didn't say anything. Schneider belched. I looked at my car down the street a few paces and started for it. I hadn't quite reached it when Fisher called, "How about some coffee?"

I put one hand against the car and leaned there, rubbing my face against my sleeve.

Coffee, hell, I thought.

But then I was thinking: But if I don't do it, it will be allowed to run down the drain, and a guy got killed in Donovan's jurisdiction, and I don't care about the guy, but he was Eloise's father, and she has got a right to know.

"Sure," I said to Fisher. "Coffee would be good."

CHAPTER 14

It was five in the morning, and outside, the dawn was trying to break through the fog. My stomach burned from the coffee I had swallowed, and my throat was dry as stale bread. Schneider was slumped on a sofa with his feet up, half-asleep. Fisher, in shirt sleeves, his tie pulled loose, was hoarse. The noise of the surf was an irregular, insistent exasperation. Nobody had said anything for three or four minutes.

Fisher finally came along with, "So it was that thing Barnes said that started all this. When I heard that Nick had a plan to wreck the organization, that was something new. He never said anything to me about it."

"Had he said anything to you about Eloise?" I asked.

"Yes. She was the thing he was really worried about."

"So am I," I said.

Fisher walked stiffly around the room, rubbing the back of his neck.

"I liked Nick Royal," he said. "I didn't like his scene—all that Fielding crap—I tried to get him to pull out. But he was blind to it—at that time—and he liked the challenge. He was a good man—tough, brilliant in his way, must have been a hell of a Marine.

"The first I heard about his fall from grace was about three months ago. 'The Old Man is going to give me the shaft,' he said. 'I'm getting too big for my pants.' He was laughing about it, but pretty soon he quit laughing. 'It looks like it's him or me,' he told me. 'He's subverting my men.' They were 'his men' by that time; he thought of them that way, and I think it was true. They had respect for him."

"Would there be any Nick Royal supporters now?" I said.

He shook his head.

"I doubt it. Politics is fickle."

"Will they be solid behind Edgar?"

"Probably not. They know who pays the bills, and they know Fielding doesn't trust anybody."

"Do they know Edgar's wife is Fielding's mistress?"

Fisher shrugged.

"If they do, that would lower Edgar a few pegs in their esteem."

"If Nick really had been able to wreck the organization," I said, "Edgar would be hurt most, wouldn't he?"

"Well, Fielding—"

"But only his pride, and he would come back."

"I suppose so."

I blinked my eyes rapidly, trying to cut a peephole through the fog.

"You say they're having this big special meeting down at the headquarters—"

"Tomorrow," Fisher said, "that is, today. I heard about it talking to Gretchen about Eloise. She wanted to get Eloise straightened out in case she had to go to the meeting herself."

"Somebody will get thrown to the wolves," I said.

"Undoubtedly," Fisher said.

I looked at the fog some more.

"Nick never said a word to you about trying to wreck the League?"

"No. The last I heard from Nick directly was in the middle of the night as he was leaving for Chicago. All he said was, 'I'm going to Chicago—check out some stuff about Eloise. Don't tell anybody, not anybody.' 'When will you be back?' I asked him, and he said, 'Don't wait up.' The next thing I knew, he was dead."

Schneider's head dropped forward. After a while he pulled one knee up, carefully retied his shoelace and put his foot back where it had been before.

"How long does it take to drive to the compound, whatever they have there?" I asked.

"This time of day—an hour and forty-five minutes, maybe two hours."

I got on my feet. It didn't feel very good, but it felt better than sitting around.

"What have you got in mind?" Fisher said.

"I guess I better make that trip," I said.

Schneider turned his head slowly and looked at me.

"They'll kill you down there," he said. "They'll cut off your head and dump the rest of you over the border."

"Yeah," I said. "Well, maybe if I have enough figured out by then, I can tip the cops and let them sweat it."

I went to Max Fisher's nearest bathroom, took off my tie and shirt and washed up. It would have been nice to have had a fresh shirt.

When I got back to the study, Schneider was up.

"I'm going along," he said.

"Think it over," I said.

"I thought it over. Let's go."

"Me, too," Max Fisher said.

"No, not you," I said. "If you want to be of real service, you might stand by, in case we yell for help."

"But what do you plan to do?"

I shrugged. I honestly couldn't tell him.

"I'll see what turns up. I got to find out a couple of things having to do with Edgar Royal."

He didn't like it too well, but he didn't argue. I guessed I could trust him. I nodded to Schneider, and we left the house.

* * * *

We drove south on the freeway, toward San Diego. It was after sunrise when we started; but the sky was overcast, and the driving was easy. Schneider slumped beside me, pulled his hat over his face and went to sleep. I was glad to have him with me and that he didn't feel talkative. But then, I remembered, he seldom did.

Somewhere north of San Diego proper we turned inland and drove south and east, most of the time through open country. It was dry and dusty, and the cultivated areas were separated by desert stretches, with few trees and no water anywhere in sight. I felt remote from the real world and was homesick for Chicago—or even Milwaukee.

Schneider woke up, making noises in his throat, opening the window to spit out of it.

"Were you in Milwaukee that day the Braves won the pennant?" I said.

"Yeah, I was. Good day."

"Great day."

"The only thing I can imagine better would be if the Cubs would win it."

"They never will."

"I guess not."

"They've got night blindness."

"In the old days—"

"There ain't any old days anymore."

"You are right."

Pretty soon I said, "Let's get out that map Fisher gave us and see where we have to go."

He got the map out, finally spotted a landmark and studied things out. The haze had gone to sea, and inland it was bright and hot.

"There's this town—not much of a town," he said, "but Fisher said there's a motel, and the compound is about three miles east of it. The compound is surrounded by a steel fence, and there are trees—those big high eucalyptus trees—all along it for a screen. It covers ten acres, and there are seventeen buildings, including an auditorium, four bunkhouses, a cafeteria, a gymnasium—"

"All right, I remember all that."

"No booze is served on the compound. Fielding doesn't hold with it."

"O.K."

"But there is a tavern in the town."

"I'm glad to hear it."

"There is only one entrance to the compound, which is a steel gate, and there is a gatekeeper on duty twenty-four hours a day."

"Uh-huh."

"How the hell do we expect to get in there?"

"When we come to it."

"If Edgar came straight down, he's inside the compound already."

"I doubt that he came straight down. I imagine there are some urgent conferences taking place at the Fielding mansion."

"Whatever you say. Anyway, it's about ten miles to this town."

"I hope there's a restaurant open."

The restaurant was part of the tavern and both were closed. A sign on the door read OPEN 8 A.M. So we had nearly an hour to wait. Nothing else was open in the town, what there was of it, except the motel, if you could call it open. We waited five minutes after ringing the bell on the manager's desk.

He had a vacancy at the front of the lot with a window from which we could watch both the highway into town and the first fifty yards of the private blacktop road that wound away toward the compound. There was nothing to obstruct the view. There wasn't that much to the town.

One of the pleasant features of the motel was a water heater and the material from which to build half a dozen cups of instant coffee. We built some and sat around with it, waiting for the restaurant to open.

"Ordinarily, according to Fisher," I said, "the group gets together for the weekend every two weeks, and between times there's a skeleton crew. Today it's a special meeting and on short notice. So I think they'll be coming in during the day, and I doubt that many have arrived yet."

"We going to the meeting?" Schneider asked.

"Not if we can help it."

"What then?"

"I want to try to cut Edgar—and Blick and that other one—what's his name?"

"Roger. Roger-babe."

"Yeah. The three of them I want to cut out and deal with."

"We go inside after them?"

"I hope we can get to them before they go inside. That means watching. I figure we can take turns, get a little sleep."

"All right," Schneider said. "Flip for the first tour?"

"I'll take the first tour. I'm not sleepy. If you'll stay up while I go to the restaurant and bring back some chow."

"Sure," he said.

So that was worked out, and so the hours went. The food I brought back from the restaurant wasn't fancy, but it was filling and hot and went down all right. Schneider was asleep two minutes after he put down the last of the bacon. I sat by the window and watched the road. In two hours, aside from three small service trucks and one gasoline tanker, there was no traffic at all. But by nine thirty, when it was time for Schneider to take over, an irregular flow of cars was in progress. Nearly all of them went on past the town, but four turned off onto the private road. None of the four carried anyone recognizable to me.

It wasn't easy to rouse Schneider; but he finally made it, and it was my turn. I was ready for sleep, and as far as I knew, I didn't toss or turn. A long time later, Schneider told me I talked in my sleep. But I didn't believe it then, and I still don't.

He got me up at eleven thirty, and we watched the traffic entering town. It was heavier than it had been at nine thirty, but it was no rush. Schneider was making sporadic tallies on a pad of white paper.

"Been counting," he said. "Since I started, forty-nine—this one makes fifty—hold it, now fifty-one—cars went down the private road. Average passenger load, one and a quarter—makes about sixty-two, sixty-three guys."

"Good counting. Anybody we know?"

"Not yet. And on account of that stop sign at the main street, you get a good look at everybody."

"Fisher estimated the total membership at something over two hundred. They're gathering slow."

"Well, Saturday morning, a lot of business people have to work."

"I thought it was against the law to work in California."

"I'll go over and get some more chow."

"Keep your ears open."

"Uh-huh."

I took up the counting from where he had left off. As he had said, it was easy enough to get a good look at every car. From either direction on the highway, each car turning into the main street of town had to come to a stop. The distance from the motel to the stop sign was not more than sixty feet. Visibility was good. In the time it took Schneider to go to the restaurant and return, five cars made the stop and the turn, and three of them continued onto the private road.

Schneider came in with a sack of food and a six pack of canned beer.

"Funny thing happened in the joint," he said.

"Yeah?"

He unpacked the groceries—hamburgers with French fries and coleslaw—and we started chewing, and drinking the beer, which was good and cold.

"Fella in there—I sat up and had a beer while I waited for the stuff—talking about the compound, the organization. He put it down pretty rough. 'Goddam Nazi finks,' was one phrase he used. Then he said there was something up—bunch of them coming through town, and it's not the regular day—maybe the cops are after them, and high time and so on. Like that."

We looked at each other, chewing. Finally my mouth cleared.

"Not straight?" I said.

He shook his head.

"Not straight, Jack. A spy."

"Did he have much of an audience?"

"Three guys, including me and the bartender."

"Well," I said, "I guess we're the only strangers in town."

He took a big bite of hamburger sandwich and nodded.

"They found us pretty quick," I said.

He shrugged.

I took a slantwise look through the window and went out to where we had parked the car. From inside I could only see the rear quarter of it. I backed and filled, turning it around to face the street and far enough out from the building so we could watch it from inside. The chances were we would have to use it in a hurry, and I didn't want anybody fooling around with it.

We finished the meal, and Schneider went to bed. He started to take his shoes off, then stopped to think, retied the laces and kept them on.

"Just keep thinking," I said.

"Yeah," he said. "Be sure to wake me up when the floor show starts."

He went to sleep—right away. There came one of those inexplicable lulls in traffic, no cars at all for as long as ten minutes, and I thought about the guy Schneider had heard in the tavern and wondered what it meant. I had picked up a lot of respect for Schneider, and my tendency was to accept his hunch. I couldn't make myself believe they would do anything about us unless we made some kind of move. The trouble with that was eventually, in some way, we would have to make a move.

By two o'clock, when it was time to wake Schneider, less than half the total company had arrived, and I decided the meeting was set for evening. The pace of the arrivals was too leisurely to suggest any action before dark. It made enough sense; too many members on short notice couldn't make advance arrangements and would show up late in the day. I told Schneider what I was thinking, and he went along with it.

"Whatever difference it makes," he said.

"Everything is more difficult in the dark," I said.

"True," he said.

I got on the bed, and it felt good to lie down, but I couldn't drop into a good sleep. The main thing bugging me was that if Schneider was right and we had been spotted, we had probably been identified, too. In some ways, we could mean more trouble than regular cops, and that could lead to a change of plans in the compound. We could hang around for ten days taking turns looking out the window and never see anything worth looking at.

"We got a telephone in here?" I said.

"Yeah," Schneider said.

"Let's call Max Fisher. I got an idea."

"It's right there," he said. "Reach for it."

Sure enough, it was on a stand beside the bed. I picked it up, and after a while somebody answered. I said I wanted to speak to Max Fisher in Los Angeles, and eventually the manager's wife figured out what directory to look at and said she would try to get him. I hung up and waited, fighting now to stay awake. In about five minutes, the phone rang, and she had Fisher on the line. He wondered what was happening.

"Nothing yet," I said. "We're at the Cozy Corner Motel and this is the phone number." I gave him the number.

"What do you need?" he asked.

It was the right way to ask the question.

"Here is what I think," I said. "I think I know what happened in Chicago, but I couldn't prove it to a kindergarten seminar. I got to find out a couple of things. It looks as if Schneider and I will have to go inside the compound to find them out. It would be silly for us—two guys—to try to make that scene without official status or help or something. So this is what I wish you would do. Ready?"

"Ready," he said.

"Call Lieutenant Donovan in Chicago—police, homicide. Keep trying till you get him personally. Ask him to call the metropolitan police headquarters nearest wherever this is—"

"San Diego," he said.

"San Diego, and tell them they can pick up two guys who killed Nick Royal in Chicago, if they will get in touch with me—Mac, that is—and Karl Schneider, at this Cozy Corner Motel—if they hurry up. This is a tricky business because of the red tape and normal suspicion and inertia and all that stuff and because I'm not sure yet that the suspects will be available at the proper moment; but if they hear it from Donovan in Chicago, they might hop to it, and we might work things out."

"All right," he said, "I've got it, I think. I'll call Lieutenant Donovan right away."

"Good, thanks—"

"There's one thing. You're not very close to San Diego. It will take them at least an hour to drive to where you are."

"Oh," I said.

"But I'll push it as hard as I can."

"O.K., do that."

I hung up. Schneider glanced at me.

"California is full of space," I said.

"Uh-huh," he said and went back to looking out the window.

I began to drift into a doze. I was in and out of it for a while and then got in deeper, and I was on the brink of sound sleep when Schneider shook me wide awake.

"Edgar Royal just made the stop sign," he said.

Even in my foggy state, I was vaguely disappointed, but I got up.

"Is he alone?" I asked.

"Just he and his shadow."

I was more specifically disappointed.

The telephone rang. I grabbed it, and it was Fisher.

"You did it already?" I said.

"I got Donovan, and he said he'd call San Diego. But it's a rough scene, Mac. I called a very high-up guy in the police in Los Angeles and told him the situation, and he said, 'If it involves Fielding's thing, these guys have got to have it absolutely wrapped up. Because no police force in southern California is going to move in on Fielding without total, secure, absolute, solid—'"

"All right, the hell with it," I said.

Schneider had the door open.

"I'll stay on it," Fisher said.

"O.K.," I said, and hung up.

"It's the green Chevy," Schneider said.

I could see it moving along the main street, which was crowded now with the late Saturday traffic.

"We go?" Schneider said.

There wasn't anything else to do anymore.

"Yeah," I said. "Let's go."

By the time we got the car onto the street, the green Chevy was reaching the end of the business district approaching the private road. We had good luck with the lights and the traffic, and although the car was not in sight when we hit the private road, we knew it would be overtakable.

We overtook it within half a mile. It was a big smooth-running model, and Edgar Royal was driving easily with one arm resting on the windowsill, not hurrying. There wasn't anything nervous about him, and this bugged me.

"He's curious about us," Schneider said quietly.

I could see Royal eyeing us in his mirror.

"He never set eyes on me," Schneider said.

"He saw me twice," I said. "But even if he doesn't remember, he'll know in a minute or so that we don't belong to the club."

"Yeah."

"Anybody behind us?"

"No," Schneider said.

"All right, don't scream if I turn off suddenly—if I find a place. We're going to do things different."

"I'm in," he said.

Ahead, Edgar had speeded up, and I let him go, even dropped back some. He disappeared around a curve, and I tried to explain my half-hatched idea to Schneider.

"It doesn't stand to reason," I said, "with this kind of operation—big compound like this, controversial, military stuff going on—that they would only have one way in and out. There has got to be another. I hope we can find it, because where I want to get to is inside, and not fool around trying to catch people on their way to the gate."

"Conditions may be better outside," Schneider said.

"Maybe."

"All right. We get inside. What do we do then?"

"I don't know."

After a minute, he said, "Good plan."

I was beginning to like him.

Cool it, I told myself. Don't have faith. Just keep moving.

CHAPTER 15

On both sides of the winding road, the eucalyptus trees grew without apparent break. On each side was a ditch at least four feet deep. Any turn-off that might lie ahead would have to be built up from the ditch. So it would be visible from a certain distance. I figured we were within a mile and a half of the compound gate. I was moving slowly enough to keep Edgar far ahead, most of the time out of sight, which was just fine. There was no problem behind, because the road was wide enough for easy passing—depending, of course, on who it was that might pass.

"Three to one," Schneider said, "an exit that returns to this road will be on our left."

It made sense. And it would probably have a one way sign up, if there were any sign at all. And the one-way direction would be against us. On the other hand, the likelihood was remote that traffic cops were patrolling the area.

"You watch left, I'll watch right," I said.

We made a sharp turn left, and about a quarter mile ahead we could see a part of the compound gate—an iron grille three car-widths broad between high fieldstone pillars. It was the left portion we could see, and I slowed to a crawl and watched Edgar's green Chevy stop for a moment, then move on to the right and disappear.

"All right, he's in," I said.

"Over there, about fifty feet," Schneider said, "on the left side, I think that's it."

"Anybody behind us?"

"No."

I gathered a little speed, and after a moment I saw what he had in mind, a passage across the ditch, where dirt lay over a five-foot galvanized drain-pipe. From our earlier angle, it appeared to head straight into tree trunks. Then I could see the break in the hedge of trees, wide enough, just barely.

There were no printed signs of any kind. There was a slight hump where the packed dirt rose on the drainpipe, and the narrow opening in the trees made room enough to make the turn. I cut it sharp left and bumped over the crossing, and we were in the trees. The dirt lane was a car-width wide and in good shape. We drove fifteen or twenty feet, and it went sharply right, heading back toward the compound tree-hedge. There was a grass meadow around us and more of it ahead, beyond where the trees thinned.

If it's all out in the open, I thought.

Stop thinking, I thought.

The getaway road began to thin out into barely discernible tracks in the grass. After the scattered trees in the turn-off clearing, we came into the open meadow, and we could see how the tracks ran back toward the eucalyptus hedge surrounding the compound.

"I do believe you're right," Schneider murmured.

There was an atmosphere of profound stillness outside the car, and it was very hot. The sun beat like a personal thing on the windows.

"It goes right along the fence," Schneider said. "If it stops, that must be the way in."

"Hang onto the thought," I said.

All of a sudden, the sun was gone. It went so fast I missed two or three heartbeats of pressure on the gas pedal.

"What happened?" I said.

"Mountains," Schneider said. "Over there. It's sunset time."

"Good."

After the first shock the quick twilight was a relief. It was easier to see, and right away it was cooler. The wind had died with the sun, and the high trees that made up the compound hedge stood still and resistant. The lane ran parallel to the hedge and the eight-foot steel-wire fence that closed it in, about twenty feet out. It was getting rougher now, and the country was piling up into hills, with periodic gullies that ran up into higher hills off to our left. There were trees in the gullies, and out of one of the cuts a thin stream of water ran and spread and disappeared in the grass.

"I can't make it out anymore," Schneider said.

"What?" I said.

"This road. I think it's about to run out."

"Say when, please."

"About thirty yards," he said.

Then I could see it myself. The ragged end of the lane melted into the high still grass ahead, and I could make out a slight curve toward the wire fence and the trees inside it. But there wasn't anything showing by way of an entrance through the fence.

The land rose on our left, and there were gullies, grown to brush, that led up to deeper gullies beyond and hills beyond that. Farther up there were brown trees, neatly scattered like planned landscapes, and brown grass underneath. And on the right, where the lane curved toward the steel fence and the hedge of trees, it was a gently sloping meadow.

"Up there," I said, pointing with one hand to the left. "Stash the car, all right?"

"You're the boss," Schneider said.

There was a gully about a hundred yards off that looked big enough. I left the faint ruts of the secret road and headed over the meadow toward the brush-filled ravine. It was bumpy, but the ground was dry and we could make it all right. It was surprising to me how quickly it got dark. By the time I hit the low, open end of the gully I had to switch on the lights for a few seconds to find my way. There wasn't anything like a road, but there was enough passable ground to work the car into the brush and low trees and feel all right about it.

"Let's see what they've got," I said.

We got out, left the car and started the walk across the meadow toward the fence.

"I wish I knew what we planned to do," Schneider said.

"Me, too," I said.

He was a good man. He didn't say anything. I wished I could have given him something to figure on, but I didn't know anything.

We got to the steel fence and stood back about five feet, looking it over. There was nothing to see beyond the thick hedge of trees, no lights, nothing.

"No trick to climb a fence like that," Schneider said, "unless it's wired."

"It's got to be wired."

"Sure."

The way it would likely be wired would be to an alarm. Probably at a touch and also probably at a firm touch. Otherwise, any stray field animal, even a mouse, could set it off, and they would be hearing alarms all night long. You would have to do something decisive to it in order to ring the bell—something like trying to climb over it.

"If we guessed right," I said, "and there's an exit around here onto that lane, there is some kind of break in it. It has got to open, anyway from inside."

"We're outside."

"Yeah," I said.

We kept looking at it. There was very little light now, and the ground and the fence and the trees were beginning to blend into one solid opaque mass.

"Got to try sometime," I said.

I walked to the fence, stroked a couple of strands of it with one finger, waited, then laid my hand against it and pushed. It gave slightly, the way tight heavy-gauge steel wire mesh gives, not readily but under considerable pressure. No alarm sounded.

"Makes no sense," I said. "There are the tracks to this point and they stop, and what the hell are they for?"

"I will tell you," Schneider said. "Once upon a time, not long ago, somebody left that other road, went through the trees and drove around here to see what he could see. He got this far, stopped, couldn't see anything, and that was the end of it."

"Great," I said. "But he must have gone back. And where is the sign that he turned around or anything like that? And besides, one set of tracks, made once, wouldn't even be visible—unless it was yesterday."

"I know it."

"Then what are you telling me?"

"Don't crowd me."

I tried not to crowd him, but I was getting impatient.

You make one bad guess, and pretty soon everything is wrong.

"There's no break in the trees either," he said. "So there can't be any way out for a vehicle right at this point."

"They've got some kind of hoist or something—drive right up to there, a steel claw comes down, picks up the car and lifts it over—"

"Cool it," he said.

I cooled it. Schneider walked along the fence about ten feet. I caught up with him and saw there was a break in the trees. The trees were farther back here, and auto tracks came through the break and turned alongside the fence. There was also in the fence what appeared to be a gate, but it was carefully contrived, and it took some studying to make out that it really was a gate and not just a flawed place in the wire. As a gate, though, it wasn't wide enough to admit a car, or even a horse. A man could get through it, though a big man might have to go sideways.

"Saw one like this once before," Schneider muttered. "They don't go in and out with cars. If somebody wants out fast—or in—he gets a ride to that point back there, or inside there, and then he walks through the gate and gets into the other vehicle."

"O.K.," I said. "They got to have their little games."

"Not just a game. It's practical. It gives a way out, but it's not enough room to let in an invasion. Old principle."

"All right," I said. "Open the gate."

"Yeah."

He ran his fingers up and down the fence where there seemed to be a flawed linkage. But then I could see that there was a thin steel bar on the back side, forming a frame. I was gazing at it, when suddenly the thing swung open.

"Easy," Schneider said. "It's a magnet. Give it a push, it opens."

"No alarm?" I said. "No warning up at headquarters?"

"Oh, probably," he said.

"Great. Let's get in there and finish up."

"Sure," he said.

I stepped through the opening and he came along. We walked up the lane close to the fence, reached the break in the trees and looked across the compound. There was still a bit of daylight, but lights had been turned on in some of the buildings on the far side.

"You bring that map?" I asked.

"Uh-huh."

He brought it out, but it was too dark to read it, and suddenly it was too late. There was the sound of a grinding motor, likely a jeep, and we moved back in the trees. The jeep turned into the break and stopped, and we could see two men in it, both wearing those white sport shirts and black suits.

"Should we check the fence?" one of them said.

"I guess so. Probably some dumb dog or something."

"Yeah."

They came off the jeep, and I nudged Schneider. They would come through the break, heading for the fence, and they would discover us at about the moment they turned the corner. They weren't carrying any visible weapons. There was no way to tell what they might have under their jackets.

Schneider nodded, and we moved along the tree-hedge, drawing apart as we went, going to meet them. They came through the break, turning toward the concealed fence opening, and there we stood. One of them jumped, but the other was cooler.

"Who—" he said.

It was a step and a half to reach them. Schneider hit his, and I hit mine almost simultaneously. Being unprepared, they both tumbled, and while they were rolling around, we got on them and hammered them quiet, not doing a lot of damage but putting them to sleep for a few seconds. I resented the fact that it hurt my hands.

"Let's get those shirts and suits," I said.

We stripped them in a matter of seconds, took off our own pants and shirts and jackets and got into the uniforms.

"Go check the jeep for chains, ropes, something," I said.

"We don't need the jeep—"

"They'll be expecting it at the place."

"O.K."

He went away, and I stood over the two we had stripped. They began to stir, but not enough to make any difference. Schneider came back with two sets of handcuffs.

"Just like downtown," he said. Then, grumbling, "Damn pants are too tight."

"Mine are too loose. Want to switch?"

"Hell with it. Find a couple small trees so we can stash these two."

One of them rolled over onto his elbows, face down.

"Listen—" he said.

"You'll be all right, Jack," Schneider said.

There were two young trees nearby, and we hauled the conscious one over there, sat him down facing one of the trees, wrapped his arms around it and snapped on the cuffs.

"You can't do this," he said.

"I know it," I said.

We got the other one, and it was harder with him because he was so limp. But we got him manacled. I picked up our jackets and put them on their shoulders.

"Keep warm," Schneider said.

The guy began to whimper about being left that way.

"How do you stand on Nick Royal?" I asked him.

"He's dead," he said.

"Yeah," I said. "Hang on. Don't let go of the tree."

"Oh, Jesus," he was saying as we went away.

"You know how to drive a jeep?" I asked Schneider.

"I drove one for four years," he said. "Get in."

As we backed onto the compound drive, he was chuckling.

"Had to do that once in the Islands," he said. "The poor bastard said the same thing—only I guess he said, 'Buddha.'"

"How do we know where to park this thing?" I said. "There must be a certain spot for it."

"The way they're organized," he said, "everything is probably marked."

"Then I hope the lights are low."

Schneider switched on the headlights. The jeep bounced some on the road. We made a sharp right turn and drove toward the compound buildings across what seemed to be a parade ground. After the turn, the road widened and led straight toward the administration building, which faced a low, barracks-like structure and some smaller outbuildings. There was a street between the barracks and the administration building. The barracks was the only large building with lights inside.

"Yeah," Schneider said. "There's a garage."

I couldn't see any garage, but when we got closer to the barracks, I made out three or four cars parked facing out of a port toward the parade ground. There were several empty spaces.

"May not be the place for the patrol car," I said.

"It will have to do," Schneider said.

There were no lights inside the carport. Schneider headed into one of the open slots, and a guy came in from a back entrance and leaned into one of the parked cars. Schneider switched off the headlights. The guy looked around and up at us for a second.

"All clear?" he said.

"Yeah," Schneider said.

"Probably some dumb dog," the guy said.

"Uh-huh," Schneider said.

The man's head went back inside the car, and we got down fast and left the carport.

"This was a bad place to come," Schneider said. "We could get killed around here."

"Just head for the dark," I said.

The darkest spot we could find was in the shadow of a small building twenty feet from the carport. It wasn't much of a place, but from its cover we could look past the barracks, across the main compound road to the administration building. The back wall of the barracks was blank except for a narrow door at one corner. Nobody seemed to make any use of it. Such foot traffic as there was came or went from the administration building, by way of high glass doors, and disappeared in front of the barracks.

"Where do we want to get?" Schneider asked.

"The administration building, I think. But we've got to check out that barracks or whatever it is."

Schneider seemed to think about it.

"Stay here," he said after a while.

He moved out from the shadow, very light on his feet, and crossed a space of thirty yards to the back of the barracks. I saw him crouching at the closed door, as if looking for a peephole. Then I saw him throw himself away from the door into the shadows at the base of the building. The door opened, light spilled from it, and a guy in white shirtsleeves stepped outside. He stood around, lit a cigarette, took a few deep breaths and went back inside, leaving the door open. I saw there was a screen door also.

Quite a lot of time went by, and Schneider began to make his way on his belly toward the open door. I ran on a long diagonal across the open space to the building and joined him, crouched low. Schneider nodded, and we both moved toward the door. He put his mouth to my ear and said, "Remember where the jeep is—in case."

I nodded. We got to within a few inches of the door, lying flat, our heads not quite in the block of light that came from it. There was a hum of male voices, a click of pool balls. Low music played. It was a recreation room. You could tell from the sound that the place was well occupied. There wouldn't be many in the administration building.

It was cold, and the ground was damp under us. I could hear Schneider breathing with a faint wheeze. I didn't like the feel of where we were.

"I wish some cops would show up," I said.

"What would we tell them?"

"By now I don't care. Tell 'em anything."

Inside, somebody laughed. A voice cut into it: "Shut up. There's the flash."

The sounds inside faded, and there were about thirty seconds of dead silence. Then a man's voice spoke above the faint buzzing of an intercom system.

"Greetings, gentlemen," it said. "This is Henry Fielding speaking. I am in my office in the administration building. I will be with you presently to say hello in person, but first I have a few announcements.

"Number one: As most of you know by now, our esteemed lieutenant, Nick Royal, is dead. This is a deep personal shock to me, as I'm sure it is to all of you. I will give you such details as I have been able to learn, when we meet tomorrow.

"Number two: Owing to circumstances beyond our control, we are unable to hold the general meeting that was called for today. It will be held at ten o'clock in the morning in the auditorium of the administration building.

"Number three: Arrangements have been made for a field trip during the weekend of July twelve to fifteen, in Mexico. We will have some interesting and important speakers and some even more interesting demonstrations. There will also be time for recreation, including fishing."

Cheers and applause. I put my mouth to Schneider's ear: "Fielding has to know who rubbed out Nick," I said. "Depending on what he does about Edgar—only place we can get what we want is that administration building."

Schneider nodded.

"Still time to go back the way we came."

He grinned at me, that gargoyle grin.

"After coming all this way?" he said.

Inside, Fielding's voice came again over the loudspeaker: "With me here in the office are Blick Delaney, whom you all know was one of Nick Royal's most trusted aides, and Roger Roby, our sergeant at arms. Blick Delaney has been made chief officer of the field, and Roger Roby is his first assistant. I know you will approve of these promotions."

More cheers and applause, but less hearty than before.

"And now," Fielding said, "I turn you over to our faithful lieutenant, Edgar Royal, Nick Royal's brother, who is your new commanding officer. Please give him your closest attention. Good night."

There was shuffling and low talk in the room. Schneider and I looked at each other.

"Time to try for it," Schneider said.

"Yeah," I said.

Edgar Royal's voice came over the loudspeaker as Schneider and I began to work our way backward along the wall of the building. After ten feet we got up, brushed off our black suits and walked around the far corner of the rec room toward the main street and the administration building. There was nobody in sight.

We paused at the street. There were windows along the front wall of the building, and we would be plenty visible crossing over.

"Walk or run?" Schneider said.

"Walk."

"Yeah," he said.

We started it, measuring our strides, cooling it, angling toward the glass doors of the administration building. My spine was a knot between my shoulder blades. The area of my kidneys burned. I was sick to my stomach and tried to blame it on those hamburgers, but I knew it wasn't so.

We made it across the street without challenge and went in by one of the glass doors. There was a Spartan-plain foyer with a gray wall opposite the doors. On the wall were picture of George Washington, next to it a large American flag, and next to that a portrait of Henry Fielding, complete with pince-nez. He looked a little like Woodrow Wilson—obviously a mistake on the part of the artist.

"How do you like that for identification?" Schneider said.

At either end of the foyer were corridors leading to the interior of the building. A sign to our left read auditorium. We went the other way. The corridor was eight feet wide, and at its far end two paneled doors with bright brass knobs were labeled headquarters—office. There were single doors at intervals along the wall to our left.

Footsteps clicked behind us, and we kept going.

"Hold on," a voice said.

We went on. The footsteps quickened. A hand grabbed my jacket at the shoulder and spun me around.

"I said, 'Hold on!'" the guy said. "You know better—Who the hell are you?"

He was carrying a rifle, complete with strap—but made of wood.

Schneider hit him once very hard in the jaw, and he went down, the gun flying away against the wall. It didn't make much noise.

"Come on," Schneider said.

We made it to the big paneled doors, got hold of the knobs and went on in.

It was a big room, for an office. The desk was the size of a small destroyer. Edgar Royal was sitting behind it, talking into a microphone. Henry Fielding sat in a high-backed chair beside him, his face on his hand, benevolent and paternal. Blick and Roger were lounging in black leather chairs facing the desk. There were half a dozen guys in white sport shirts standing at attention with those wooden guns.

The lull following our entrance lasted about four seconds. They just stared at us. Edgar Royal looked up, then back at his prepared speech, and went on reading. Fielding stood up.

"We're making an arrest," Schneider said, "in the murder of Nick Royal. Just hold still—"

Blick Delaney moved first. He did it deceptively, coming out of his chair almost lazily, one hand behind him. His arm went up, and I saw something in his hand and ducked when he threw it at me. It hit the wall behind me with a metallic ring, but I never did find out exactly what it was. As I recovered from ducking, I saw Henry Fielding disappear through a narrow door in the wall.

Schneider was going over the desk to get at Edgar Royal, who was trying to club him with the mike. They both fell down behind the desk as the six-man honor guard, or whatever it was, swarmed over me. They were jammed too close together, and the wooden guns were only a nuisance to them. They kept banging their weapons against each other's. I crouched low under their weird arm-dance and went for their bellies. I decked two, and a third one tripped over one of them, and I hit him in the back of his head as he went down.

Somebody stumbled heavily against me. It was Schneider, and he fell before I could grab him. As he went down, one of the riflemen clubbed him in the head. I hit the soldier in the nose and kicked another one, and things cleared for a few seconds. Schneider was on his back, but so were four of the soldiers. I saw Roger Roby speaking calmly into the microphone, but I couldn't hear what he said. I couldn't see Blick anywhere. One of the remaining soldiers came at me with both hands working and got me into the wall, pounding me in the soft low place. I shoved him off and suddenly, unbelievably, came the sound of far-off sirens. The guy came back, and I kicked him in the right shin and nearly broke my hand on his jaw. He went away. Schneider was trying to get up. I was sweat-blinded and couldn't find the action. The sirens rose again, closer now.

"Go!" a voice said.

It sounded like Blick. I shook my eyes clear, and five of them were on the floor, along with Schneider. Edgar Royal had disappeared. Blick and Roger and the last of the honor guard were squeezing out through that narrow door. Outside the sirens were screaming down the main street of the compound.

Schneider will be all right, I promised myself. Be all right, Schneider.

I went after Blick and Roger. The door was closed, and I yanked it open and fell down a short flight of stairs onto a landing heavy with the smell of dusty fabric. It was an entrance to the auditorium stage. I got on my feet, fought my way past the curtains and onto the stage. The three of them were going out on the far side, under a night-light marking the stage door. I got to it as it was closing, and they were on a ramp outside, fighting their way into a jeep like the one Schneider and I had stolen.

"Stay here," Roger said to the tin soldier, kicking at him. "You're in the clear. Stay with the others."

It told me quite a lot. The soldier stumbled backward, looking bewildered, and I jumped into the back end of the jeep as it pulled away. The soldier shouted. Roger, in the front seat, turned and saw me and grabbed for me. I hit him on the top of the head, and he ducked down, groping for something. Blick was driving it hard, across the main street, then bumping out over the parade ground, heading across the field toward the secret exit. I took one glance as we passed and saw some squad cars on the street and guys with helmets and guns getting organized.

The jeep was bouncing and swerving badly, and I had to spread my legs to keep from falling. Roger came up with a nightstick and swung it at me. I grabbed it, and we both held on. Roger came over the seat to get at me. I jerked the nightstick away from him, but the jeep swerved sharply, and I dropped the stick in order to grab Roger. His footing was better than mine, and on the next swerve he got his knee in my belly and shoved, and I went over the side. It felt like running into a brick wall at top speed. I managed to roll, but my head hit a hard thing and stunned me black.

I couldn't have been out for long. When I came around, there was still a lot of commotion up at the compound. I got on my feet and thought it over and decided not to return. The quarry was gone anyway, and there was nothing I could do for the cops. Besides, I wasn't sure I ought to be discovered in the midst of it. I was wearing one of their suits.

I found my way to the high trees and the break between them and onto the lane that led to the exit. The two guys we had stripped were still sitting there, handcuffed and helpless. One of them said, "Hey, cut us loose."

"I lost the key," I said. "Be patient."

He started swearing at me in a high-pitched, whiny voice, as I went on to the exit, found out where the latch was and let myself out into the field. It took me about five minutes to get where we had stashed the car. It took another five to work up enough juice to start it, back it out of the place and find the way back toward town. I drove very wildly, veering all over the field. A couple of times I got sick and had to stop and use the open window.

The main street of the town was deserted, and most places were closed. I drove erratically for a couple of blocks, tried to turn into a closed gas station and hit a steel post at a speed of thirty-five miles an hour; the car went dead. It shocked me into a temporary state of alert. I managed to get out of the car and walk steadily enough down the street to the motel. I went to the manager's office and banged the door till he got up and looked out. I told him where I wanted to go.

"What's your name?" he said.

I told him, propping myself up with both arms in his open doorway. He had to check to make sure. Finally, he picked a key off a rack and gave it to me.

"Hey," he said, as I started away, "what's going on up at the compound?"

"I don't know," I said. "I been on a hard drunk—got to go to bed."

"Where's your friend?" he said.

"The cops picked him up."

I hope, I thought. I hope they did.

He let me in, and I found the bed and fell on it. After a while I got up and found the telephone, put in a call to Max Fisher and hung up. I fell asleep, and I don't know exactly when the call came through, but it was later.

"Everybody got away," I told Fisher. "The cops came."

"I know," he said. "I finally got somebody to push them into a move. Then Schneider called me."

"Where's Schneider?"

"In the hospital. He'll be all right, but he's got something broken."

"I smashed my car," I said.

"Where are you?"

I told him.

"I'll come and get you," he said.

"O.K. I got to sleep awhile. But come by daybreak. We've got to make a call."

"Where?"

"Mr. Henry Fielding," I said.

"All right. Daybreak."

I fell asleep. Now and then I would wake up, but most of the time I slept.

CHAPTER 16

The sun was very bright on the water, and the curving beach was white. They were working out horses in the surf, and the horses and riders were black moving lumps at this distance. The brown grass on the hill was dry and stiff, there was no wind, and it was hot in the car. Halfway down the arroyo to our left, the Fielding mansion was a cluster of white-walled Spanish buildings with red tile roofs, enclosed on three sides by eucalyptus trees. There was sunlight on the veranda of the main house, and it wasn't hard to picture an early California don, looking down the arroyo to where the horses were plunging in the water. But he wouldn't care much for it now, I decided, with that highway between and the sun glinting nervously in flashes from the steady two-way traffic between Los Angeles and San Diego.

"There it is," Max Fisher said. "How do you want to do it?"

"I don't want to do it. I don't want to have anything to do with it. But I guess I've got to."

"Because of the girl?"

"Yeah—and Donovan—and my own satisfaction. You don't have to bother with it. If you'll drop me—"

"Come on," he said, "I'm in it all the way."

"It may get hot, if Blick and that other one are down there."

"Maybe. But if they came for protection—"

"Their protection is fickle."

He looked at me but didn't ask any questions. He was a good man.

"Let's go get it done," I said.

He let the car drift downward into the road that led to Fielding's house. I wondered whether Schneider felt comfortable in the hospital.

A rugged one, I thought. An authentic, durable tough guy.

The road curved, and for a minute we couldn't see the house, only those high, fragile eucalyptus. I moved my hands, wishing I had something to use them for—not that they were worth much at the moment. I flexed my fingers and thought maybe the left one was broken, but I didn't really believe it.

Then the road switched back, and we were close now and could see the parking area at the garage. Between the garage and the house a private hedge partly enclosed a patio and swimming pool. It was the first time I had seen it by day and it was nice to see, a gracious, leisurely way of life. I noticed that it was impossible to see the beach and the horses from this point. In the old days—

But that was the old days when there was a real life.

I laughed out loud.

"Take it easy," Fisher said. "Shall we enter by the front or the rear?"

"Whichever's the most direct route," I said.

The garage door was closed, and I looked through a screened vent and saw a black Cadillac, a light-colored Buick and a jeep. The jeep was familiar.

We took the passage beside the garage and came into the patio. Sunshine glinted on the pool water, and on the firm, shapely legs and thighs of Gretchen Royal, stretched out on a chaise at poolside. Her naked diaphragm rose and fell evenly, and she appeared to be asleep. But within seconds of our quiet approach, moving only her lips, she said, "Who is it?"

I glanced at Max Fisher, who said, "It's me, Mrs. Royal."

"Oh," she said. "Something to sign?"

"No, nothing like that."

She lay still a few seconds, then shrugged her way onto her elbows and looked at us. She was wearing very dark sunglasses, and if she registered any shock at seeing me, it was not apparent.

"What does he want?" she said.

"We'd like to speak with Eloise," I said.

"Who wouldn't?" she said.

"She's not here?"

"Oh, yes, she's here—somewhere. But she's not communicating with anybody, least of all me."

"Well," I said, "could you let me try?"

She swung her good-looking legs over the side of the chaise, got to her feet and did something to her hair.

"I remember you from somewhere," she said.

"Chicago," I said.

"Oh, yes. About Eloise, I don't know. She's at home; everything is straightened out."

I looked at Max Fisher, and he looked at the wall on the far side of the swimming pool. It was a white plaster wall with bougainvillea growing over it. It was a nice wall, I thought.

"Everything," I said, "but the murder of Nick Royal."

"You think Eloise can help with that?" Gretchen said.

"I think maybe she can."

She opened her red mouth, then closed it and snatched up a towel from the chaise.

"If you can find her," she said.

She flipped the towel over her shoulders and walked away and through a side door into the house. Max Fisher and I looked at each other and looked at other things. "Motherhood," Max said.

"I wonder where the lieutenants are this morning," I said.

"Funny they would come here, if they're hot—the most obvious place—"

"They don't know yet how hot they really are, and besides, where else would they go? They ratted on their first boss when they turned on Nick, and then they dumped Edgar when Gretchen dumped him, and so Fielding is all they've got left. Fielding, that is, or Gretchen."

"Well, say the two of them did for Nick Royal—"

"Oh, they surely did."

"Can Eloise help prove it?"

I nodded.

"She can place them near the scene, near enough maybe. She already told Schneider and me. I just want her to tell somebody else."

"Then we'd better find her in a hurry."

"Yeah, but when you hurry, you attract attention."

There was movement in the house at the other end of the pool. Henry Fielding came into a breakfast room with high French doors that stood open. He was wearing a long-sleeved white sport shirt and black trousers. He sat down at the table and propped up a newspaper. A Mexican girl in a white uniform brought him a plate and went away. Fielding took no notice of her. He didn't take any notice of us either, just went on reading his paper.

"*El patrón*," Max Fisher muttered.

"What does that mean?"

"The boss."

I don't know whether it was our voices or some other momentary disturbance, but Fielding looked up from his paper and turned his face toward the patio. If he saw us, it didn't register. He looked out and went back to the paper.

Not a bad technique, I thought. Let 'em come all the way on with it. If it's a bad scene, reach for the phone, or yell for somebody.

But he wasn't reaching for the phone now.

We walked along the edge of the pool toward the house, and Fielding took no notice whatsoever. We got all the way to the open door and stopped, the way you do, waiting to be acknowledged, but there wasn't any acknowledgment. We looked at each other and Max shrugged. I looked at Henry Fielding. He had a slight vertical crease in his forehead that ran down to the nosepiece of his pince-nez. Otherwise his face was unlined and clean, almost benign in its smoothness.

"Good morning, Mr. Fielding," I said.

The crease in his head deepened a little, his eyebrows twitched, and his gaze shifted to another point on the page.

The hell with him, I thought.

"Got to make a deal with you," I said. "In return for your man Blick and the other one, Roger-babe, and in return also for a few minutes of conversation with Eloise Royal—in return for these things—"

He was looking at me now, head on.

"Yes?" he said.

"We'll go away and leave you alone."

His mouth moved again.

"I remember you," he said.

"I'm glad," I said. "That could save some time."

His mouth thinned. He was facing the kind of challenge he enjoyed. And he could go at it only one way—straight. He was so straight you could have used him for a plumb bob.

Which might be fun, too, I thought.

"Do I owe you any money?" he said.

"No," I said.

"Then I can't imagine what you want, unless it's to try and destroy my organization, which you may not find so easy."

I blinked.

"I think your organization is in charge of its own destruction," I said. "May we speak with Eloise?"

"You'll have to see her mother about that."

"We saw her mother, but she wasn't much help."

He shrugged, as if to return to his reading.

"I can't help you, I'm afraid."

The girl in the white uniform came in through a swinging door, half-crossed the room, then turned and went back where she had come from.

She's going to place a call, I thought. Somebody bugging the boss.

Over my left shoulder somewhere, a door opened. I turned, and Eloise stepped out of a room halfway along the pool. She was wearing a bikini with a pattern of blue polka dots, and she had a towel over her shoulder. She was at the edge of the pool when she noticed us.

"Hello," she said.

I waved at her. Footsteps sounded beyond her, and Blick and Roger came into the patio from beyond the garage and stopped at the far end of the pool, looking at us. After a moment they moved, Roger to the right corner of the pool, Blick to the left. Blick stood at a point at which Eloise was directly between him and me. He had a snub-nosed revolver in his hand, not pointing at anything in particular. I felt duty-bound to keep my eyes on him, so

I don't know what kind of signal passed between him and Henry Fielding, but the next time Blick spoke, he said, "You—both of you—get out. Split."

"Now, Blick," Eloise said, "shut up."

"Eloise," Fielding said sternly, "go back in the house."

Her nose went high in the air, and she threw the towel down in a feminine rage.

"No! I came for a swim, and I'm going to swim."

She dived in, making plenty of splash.

"Stick close," I said to Max. "We'll call on Mr. Fielding."

I turned my back on Blick, nudged Max and we walked in a direct line toward Fielding, who watched us with a tight face but without apparent concern. We went along the table edge and stopped behind him, so there wasn't much Blick could do with that gun at that distance without the risk of sending Henry Fielding to eternity.

"This is called, I believe," Fielding intoned, "breaking and entering."

"Yes, sir," I said. "Max, find a telephone and call the police. Tell them we've broken and entered Mr. Henry Fielding's premises."

Max looked uncertain, then moved away.

"Just a moment," Fielding snapped. "That's very funny."

Fisher stopped. I looked at Eloise splashing back and forth in the pool and wondered whether there was a real world for her in there.

"What do you want us to do, Mr. Fielding?" Blick said.

I was glad the question was not addressed to me. It was a bad one.

"Come in here, both of you," Fielding said.

"Tell him to put the gun away," I said.

After a pause, Fielding went me one better.

"Put the gun down and come in," he said.

Blick looked longingly at the gun, then stooped and put it down on the concrete at the pool's edge. He nodded at Roger, and they came toward the house on opposite sides of the pool. Eloise had stopped swimming and was clinging to the edge with both hands, watching us. Blick and Roger stopped at the open door and stood looking in.

"Come inside," Fielding said. "Sit down at the table. It's time for a conference."

Brother, I thought.

Blick and Roger sat down across from Fielding.

"I'll stand, if it's all the same to you," I said.

"Now, then," Fielding said, picking a cue out of the air, "what's this nonsense about killing somebody?"

"Not just somebody," I said. "Nick Royal. Remember him?"

"Of course."

I looked at Eloise, who was still in the pool, working her way hand over hand, slowly, toward our end of the patio. From where I stood the world seemed totally unreal. I couldn't bring myself to do the thing in her presence.

"Max," I said, "go ahead and call the cops. I don't want to have to go through it more than once."

Max walked away. Eloise clung to the edge of the pool with her tiny white hands, and her long hair was plastered close around her miniature face.

"Listen, Mr. Fielding—" Blick said.

"Patience, Blick," Fielding said. "I'm sure everything will be worked out satisfactorily."

I guess it was the only way he knew to keep his cool. It wasn't a good way for Blick.

"What do you mean, 'worked out'?" he said. He was halfway up on his feet, leaning heavily on the table toward Fielding. "You going to offer them *money* or something?"

Fielding's face was cold as window glass in an abandoned building.

"Don't be stupid," he said. "Nobody has even begun to prove that you and Roger killed Nick Royal."

From the pool, her voice ringing over her clinging hands, Eloise shouted, "Somebody will! They beat up Karl Schneider in that place. I saw them! Then they killed my father!"

We stared at her. Max Fisher came back from wherever he had found the phone. The side door of the house opened, and Gretchen Royal came out, dressed for the street. Eloise looked round at her, then pushed away from the edge and swam with long, lazy strokes toward the far end. Gretchen Royal looked into the breakfast room.

"Henry," she said, "I'm going downtown—"

"In a few minutes, my dear," Fielding said.

She stood where she was. Everybody tended to do whatever Henry Fielding commanded. Everybody except Eloise. At the end of the pool, she hoisted herself up to the concrete, her arms stiffening, one leg lifting, her body swinging lightly till she was seated with her arms hugging her knees, gazing toward us from her great distance. Her mother stooped, picked up the towel Eloise had thrown down and moved as if to take it to her. Then she changed her mind and dropped it. I walked out there.

"The police are coming for Blick and Roger," I said to Gretchen. "I guess you'd better be ready to go with them."

Her eyes widened, and her mouth drew out thin. Nothing much else changed. It wasn't really such a good-looking face, I decided, at close range.

"Whatever for?" she said.

"Well, it was really you, wasn't it, who arranged for the assassination of Nick Royal? Blick and Roger just went through the motions. You thought it out."

"You must be out of your—"

"Yeah," I said.

Her eyes were doing various things, but she didn't look at anything but me.

"You've got to be—why would I?" she said. "I could only lose—"

All the things they say.

"The story of your recent life," I said, "is all about how you worked your way up in the League for Good Government—for your own ends. Nick Royal was big in the beginning, and you stuck with him. But Nick got too big for his pants, and Edgar moved in, so you switched to him. But even Edgar was only a station on the way. There was Henry Fielding. He's where the real security is. He's the one with the big money, and he's in charge. When you knew Nick was really finished, you could concentrate on getting rid of Edgar and moving on. And you got your chance, unexpectedly, all of a sudden in Chicago. I stood there and heard you get it, by telephone, when Ray Barnes called and told you Nick was in town. And you knew Nick was trying to get Eloise away from you, and you couldn't let that happen. You needed her—"

"No! I did not involve Eloise for one minute—"

"You sent out those two hatchet men, and they beat Schneider up, and then they went down the street and took care of Nick—"

"It was Edgar," she said. "It was all his idea. Edgar wanted Nick out of the way—"

"Sure he did," I said. "But not the way you did. Nick was only an insubordinate nuisance to Edgar. Edgar didn't know Nick planned to wreck the organization. But I think you did, and Fielding did, and that's what caused all that shenanigans about the bill for those guns."

Eloise was on her hands and knees on the concrete beside the pool, her head hanging down, as if she were exhausted. Her long hair glowed strangely in the sun.

It will be over soon, I thought, and it will become unreal, and then it will be easier. Maybe.

I went on, trying to end it for good. Gretchen was looking beyond me now, toward the breakfast room. I wished I could keep my eyes on Blick and Roger, but there was Max Fisher—

"You could make it look as if Edgar had ordered the killing," I said, "but you could never have made it stick. Edgar didn't know Nick was in Chicago. But you knew. You knew it before anybody else, and I heard you get the information with my own ears. I saw you crook your finger at Roger and then at Blick. It didn't mean anything much then; but it means a lot now, and it will send you away, believe it."

Like a wounded animal, Eloise was crawling slowly toward the corner of the pool. Far off on the highway a remote whine of sound rose. Sirens. But there are always sirens. Gretchen Royal's eyes were squeezed out of shape now. She backed off a few steps.

"No," she said, but it was only a moan.

"It was all neat and planned," I said. "Hurried, but planned. The only happenstance was that I happened to be on the scene when they took care of Nick. That worked to their advantage at first, but eventually, the way these things go—"

"No!" This time it was a scream.

Gretchen turned from me and started to run unsteadily on her high heels toward the passage beside the garage. I didn't really see all of what happened. It was as if someone were telling me about it. Eloise had reached the place where Blick had put his gun down at Fielding's command. I didn't see her pick it up. I saw Eloise on her knees with the gun in both hands, and I saw Gretchen stumble and fall forward and roll over once, and it was quiet. And then I heard the report. And next I heard Max Fisher shout and running steps. Crouching, I got to Eloise, and we both fell, me trying to get hold of the gun and not fall on top of her. Then I was on my knees, pivoted, and she was curled up in a ball somewhere under me, and Blick had got two-thirds of the length of the pool in his flight. When I shot him, he swerved and tried to keep running; but the slug was too heavy, and he lost his balance and fell into the pool. Nearby was the sound of cars and doors slamming, and the police were coming in from beyond the garage. Eloise was shaking, and I got hold of her and held her tight, and I remember saying out loud over and over, "It didn't happen; it isn't real; it didn't happen—"

It was real, of course, but I don't think it's real to Eloise anymore. Gretchen lived through it, and they sent her up for a few years; but they didn't do anything harsh to Eloise.

Fielding escaped, too, but he didn't have any organization left, and I will say for him that he provided well for Eloise. He did what he could for Blick and Roger, too, but there wasn't much to be done for them when the case got put together. It was a good strong case. Even Donovan admitted it—grudgingly.

I went to see Schneider in the hospital, and I saw him in Chicago once for a few minutes, but I haven't seen him since.

www.ingramcontent.com/pod-product-compliance
Lightning Source LLC
Chambersburg PA
CBHW020656180626
46816CB00003B/1318